"We want that gun, Mason," said Sergeant Holcomb.

"What gun?" asked Perry Mason.

"The gun that killed Penn Wentworth."

"I haven't got it."

"That's what you say."

Mason's face darkened. "That," he announced with cold finality, "is what I say."

"Okay," Sergeant Holcomb said. "We wanted to give you an out. If we have to do it the hard way, we can do it the hard way."

And with that, Sergeant Holcomb reached into a bag and produced evidence that could send Perry Mason to jail and his client to the gas chamber!

THE CASE OF THE POSTPONED MURDER
was originally published by
William Morrow and Company, Inc.

ERLE STANLEY
GARDNER
THE CASE OF THE
POSTPONED MURDER

PUBLISHED BY POCKET BOOKS NEW YORK

THE CASE OF THE POSTPONED MURDER

William Morrow edition published 1973
POCKET BOOK edition published April, 1974

This POCKET BOOK edition includes every word contained
in the original, higher-priced edition. It is printed from
brand-new plates made from completely reset, clear, easy-to-
read type. POCKET BOOK editions are published by POCKET
BOOKS, a division of Simon & Schuster, Inc., 630 Fifth
Avenue, New York, N.Y. 10020. Trademarks registered
in the United States and other countries.

L

Standard Book Number: 671-77894-3.
Library of Congress Catalog Card Number: 72-1344.

Publisher's Note

The manuscript for *The Case of the Postponed Murder* was one of two full-length Perry Mason novels left in Erle Stanley Gardner's pending file at the time of his death in 1970. Although the work was written earlier and set aside, the publishers believe it was ready for publication. But it should be noted that the author had not done his usual final-draft polishing and checking.

Cast of Characters

Verb

■

1

PERRY MASON pushed himself slightly back from the desk and turned so that he was facing the young woman who had seated herself in the client's big overstuffed leather chair. Della Street, his secretary, handed him the confidential information card on which had been typed:

NAME . . . . Sylvia Farr
AGE . . . . Twenty-six
ADDRESS . . . . North Mesa, Calif., 694 Chestnut St. Temporarily located at Palmcrest Rooms. Telephone number Hillview 6-9390.
NATURE OF BUSINESS About sister.
COMMENTS . . . . When she opened her purse for compact, noticed a wad of folded bills and several pawn tickets.—D.S.

Mason turned the card face down on the desk and said, "You wanted to see me about your sister, Miss Farr?"

"Yes."

"Smoke?" Mason asked, raising the cover of his office humidor.

"Thanks. I have my own brand." She took a new package from her purse, tore open a corner, extracted a cigarette, and leaned forward for his match.

"All right," Mason said, settling back in his chair. "What about your sister?"

"She's disappeared."

"Ever do it before?"

"No."

"What's her name?"

"Mae."

"Married?"

"No."

"What about the disappearance?"

Sylvia Farr gave a quick, nervous laugh and said, "It's hard for me when you shoot questions at me. Could I tell you in my own way?"

"Certainly."

"Well, we live in North Mesa, and—"

"Just where is North Mesa?" Mason interrupted. "I don't recall the place."

"You wouldn't," she said. "It's in the northern part of the state, off the main highways. It's awfully rural. There hasn't been any building activity for years. We did manage a new post office, but that doesn't mean anything in particular."

"So much for North Mesa," Mason said with a smile. "Now how about Mae?"

"Mae," she said, "left North Mesa over a year ago. It was the opposite of the conventional, short-story situation. She was the household drudge. I was the— Well, I was considered prettier, not," she added quickly, with a deprecating smile, "that that means much in North Mesa.

"But you know the conventional setup. I should have been the one to get impatient at the small-town stuffiness and head for the big city, try to crash the movies, wind up making a living waiting on tables in a cheap restaurant, then marry a prince charming—or go broke and return home, disillusioned, bitter, and cynical, to find that my homely sister had married the local undertaker, had three children, and was known all over the countryside for her wonderful disposition and fine apple pies."

Mason's eyes twinkled. "Mae," he asked, "didn't run true to form?"

8

"I'll say she didn't. She got fed up with North Mesa and decided she was going to see the world."

"Where is she now?"

The laughter faded from Sylvia Farr's eyes. "I don't know," she said.

"Where was she when you heard from her last?"

"Here."

"Was she working?"

"She'd had several jobs," Sylvia Farr said guardedly. "I think she tried to make up for some of the things she had lost in North Mesa. She formed a few friendships and enjoyed them immensely. She became quite a play-girl."

"Older than you or younger?" Mason asked.

"A year and a half older. Don't misunderstand me, Mr. Mason. She knew what she was doing. . . . But what I mean is that her attitude changed. In North Mesa, there was no animation about her. She seldom laughed. She felt she was just marking time there while life was slipping through her fingers, and her actions showed it. After she came to the city, she apparently had an entirely different outlook. Her letters really sparkled. They were quite clever, and . . . Well, I didn't dare show all of them to Moms. I remember that Mae said that in the city a girl had to play with fire and that the art of keeping fingers from getting burnt was not to try to control the fire but to control the fingers."

"When did you hear from her last?"

"A little over two months ago."

"What was she doing then?"

"She was working as secretary to a man in the stationery business, but she didn't give me the address of the firm. She was staying at the Pixley Court Apartments, and she seemed to be having a wonderful time."

"You have a letter?" Mason asked.

"No. I destroyed all of her letters—that is, nearly all of them. She used to write me things in confidence. Occasionally, she'd write a letter for Moms to read, but they were mostly little notes."

"Did she ever come back to North Mesa after she left?" Mason asked.

"Yes, she was back about six months ago, and I was never so flabbergasted in my life. I've never seen such a complete change in any human being. Her complexion was never good, and her hair was inclined to be coarse and dry. Her features aren't what you'd call beautiful, but, my heavens, to see what she'd done to herself! Her clothes were smart. Her complexion was a lot better. Her eyes danced. She'd been taking care of her hair and her hands, and she was full of wisecracks and all the latest slang. She made us North Mesa girls feel hopelessly out of things.

"You know, Mr. Mason, I'm not the moody type. I take things as they come and live life as I find it, but I never felt as blue as when Mae had left and we settled back into the old rut. Things weren't so bad while she was there. Just being around her made all of the girls feel sort of urban and sophisticated, but after Mae left, the steam was all out of the boiler, and we couldn't carry on. . . ."

"I think I understand," Mason said. "I think we've covered the preliminaries fairly well, Miss Farr."

"Well," Sylvia Farr went on hastily, "a month or so ago I wrote Sis, and she didn't answer. Then I sent her another letter about two weeks ago, and the letter was returned with a note from the apartment house saying that she'd moved and had left no forwarding address."

"She sounds as though she'd developed an ability to take care of herself," Mason said. "I would hardly think there was any cause for worry."

"In her last letter," Sylvia Farr explained, "she mentioned a Mr. Wentworth who had a yacht. I understand he's a gambler and rather wealthy. She'd been out on the yacht with him and wound up the letter by saying some-

10

thing like this: 'Good Heavens, Sis, if you come to the city, lay off of people like Penn Wentworth. What I've told you about playing with fire doesn't fit him. He goes through life taking what he wants, not asking for it. You can't control either the fingers or the fire with men like that.' "

Mason said, somewhat impatiently, "Your sister isn't the first girl in the world to find that you can't make hard and fast rules about playing with fire, as she called it. You don't need a lawyer, Miss Farr. You need a private detective if you need anyone. If you'll take my advice, you'll return to North Mesa and forget all about it. Your sister is able to take care of herself, and the reason she has failed to communicate with you is undoubtedly because she doesn't want you to know where she is. The police can tell you that this frequently happens. If you want a good detective, the Drake Detective Agency in this same building has several very skillful operatives, and you can absolutely trust the discretion and honesty of Mr. Paul Drake, the head of the agency. He does my work."

And Mason swung about in his chair as an indication that the interview was terminated.

Sylvia Farr crossed over to the desk and stood looking down at him. "Please, Mr. Mason," she said, with desperation in her voice, "I know it sounds silly. I just couldn't tell it the way it was. I can't make you see Sis the way I know her. I tell you I *know* this is something different. I think—think—that she's dead, been murdered."

"What makes you think that?" Mason asked.

"Oh, just several things, knowing her and—because of things she said in that last letter."

"You didn't keep that letter?"

"No."

Mason said, "If you're absolutely convinced in your own mind that there's something seriously wrong, go to the police. They'll investigate. You may not be pleased with what you find out."

"But I want you to investigate this, Mr. Mason. I want you to...."

"All I could do," Mason said, "would be to hire a detective agency. You could do that just as well yourself and save yourself money. I presume money means something to you, doesn't it, Miss Farr?"

"Yes, it does," she said. "But Sis means more to me than money, and I just know there's something wrong."

Mason said, "Go see Paul Drake. In all probability, one of his operatives can locate your sister within twenty-four hours. If it turns out your sister is in any difficulty and she needs legal help, I'll still be available."

Della Street said, "This way, Miss Farr. I'll take you to Mr. Drake's office."

2

PAUL DRAKE, long and loose-jointed, entered Mason's private office with the familiarity born of years of intimate association, and said, "Hi, Perry. Hi, Della. How's tricks?"

He crossed over to the client's chair, swung around so he was seated crosswise in the seat, and let his legs hang over one of the arms. "Thanks for the case, Perry," he said.

"What case?"

"The girl you sent me yesterday."

"Oh, you mean Miss Farr?"

"Uh huh."

"Any money in it?" Mason asked.

"Oh, so-so. Enough to cover a preliminary investigation and report. I figured it shouldn't take over three or four hours to locate the girl."

"Find her?" Mason asked.

"No, but I found out a lot about her."

Mason grinned and reached for the cigarette humidor. "Smoke, Paul?" he asked.

"No, thanks," Drake said. "I'm chewing gum today."

Mason turned to Della Street. "He has something on his mind, Della. When things are coasting along, he smokes cigarettes and sits in the chair like a civilized human being. When you see him tie himself up in knots like a snake with a stomachache, you know he has something on his mind. And chewing gum is another infallible sign."

Drake tore the cellophane end off a package of gum and fed three sticks into his mouth, one after another, rolled the wrappers into a tight ball, and tossed them into Mason's wastebasket. "Perry," he said, "I want to ask you a question."

Mason flashed Della Street an obvious wink. "Here it comes, Della," he said.

Drake said, "No kidding, Perry, you did call the turn on me."

"I know I did," Mason said. "What is it, Paul?"

"Why the devil did you interest yourself in that girl's case?"

"I didn't."

"You didn't *take* it," Drake said, "but from what she told me, you must have given her quite a bit of time."

"Did she think so?" Mason asked.

"No," Drake said. "She was sore. She thought you'd thrown her out on her ear. I explained to her that you were one of the highest-priced trial lawyers in the city and that darn few people ever got as far as your private office. That smoothed her down some."

Mason said, "I darn near took her case at that, Paul."

"That's the way I figured it. Why?"

Mason grinned and said, "You found the sister was in a fair-sized mess of trouble, didn't you, Paul?"

The detective nodded, watching Mason warily.

"A fugitive from justice?" Mason asked.

"Nope," Drake said. "Forgery."

"I thought so," Mason said.

Della Street looked at the lawyer curiously. Drake said, "Come on, Perry. Give me a break. How did you figure it?"

The lawyer's eyes narrowed somewhat as they looked past the detective. "Darn it, Paul," he said. "I wish I didn't take such a keen interest in people and in mysteries. If there'd been just a little more mystery about that case, I'd have taken it and found myself donating five thousand dollars' worth of work for a fifty-dollar fee."

"What was the mystery?" Drake asked.

"Did you locate Mae Farr?" Mason countered.

"No, we can't find her."

Mason made a gesture with his hand as though tossing something onto the big desk in front of him. "There," he said, "is your answer."

"What do you mean, Perry?"

Mason said, "Look at the setup. This girl comes to see us about her sister. Her sister has disappeared. She thinks her sister is in some sort of trouble, doesn't know anything at all about what it might be, but is filled with vague forebodings.

"Notice the way she's dressed—shoes that are the best on the market, a skirt and jacket smart in design but not new, a coat that apparently *is* new, of the cheapest sort of material cut along flashy lines with a fur collar and trim which looks as though it came direct from an alley cat."

"Well," Drake asked as Mason hesitated, "what's the answer?"

Mason waved back the question with a quick gesture. "Her nails," he said, "were manicured carefully. Her hair was slicked back. Her face had very little makeup on it. There was virtually no lipstick on her mouth, and

14

then to clinch matters, her purse was full of money—and pawn tickets."

Drake, nervously chewing away at his gum, looked across at Della Street, then back to Mason, and said, "I don't get you, Perry. You're leading up to something, but hanged if I know what."

Mason said, "It's a column of figures that doesn't add up, that's all. What does a country girl do when she goes to the city? Puts on her best clothes, tries to look her best. The country girls—the good-looking ones—are the ones who try to look sophisticated. They're the ones who go heavy on makeup when they're calling on a lawyer. They're particularly careful to have their hair done as soon as they get to the city."

"She was worried," Drake said. "She didn't have time to go to a hairdresser."

"She had had time to get her nails manicured," Mason said, "and she'd been to a hairdresser. Her hair was pulled back to make her look as plain and unsophisticated as possible. A country girl would have economized on shoes, and put what she saved into getting a better coat, unless she was the type who liked that kind of a coat. In that event, she wouldn't have ever had the shoes Miss Farr was wearing. The coat didn't go with the clothes. The coat didn't go with the shoes. The hair didn't go with the nails. The face didn't go with the story."

Drake chewed away at the gum with nervous rapidity, then suddenly straightened in the chair. "Cripes, Perry, you don't mean that she . . . that she was . . ."

"Sure, she was," Mason said. "She was a fugitive from justice. She wanted a lawyer to pull some chestnuts out of the fire. She didn't dare use her right name, so she posed as sister Sylvia."

"I," Drake announced slowly and impressively, "will be damned. I believe you're right, Perry."

"Of course I'm right," Mason said, as though dispos-

15

ing of a matter which was entirely elementary. "That's why I almost took her case. I wondered what kind of character she possessed, what sort of a scrape she was in, what mental quirk had given her the resourcefulness and ingenuity to think up that approach. Most girls would either have sought refuge in tears or hysterics or would have been hard-boiled enough to brazen the whole thing out. She wasn't particularly hard-boiled. She looked as though she knew her way around. She was frightened, but she wasn't giving way to tears. She was self-reliant and, all in all, pretty resourceful. She'd hocked all her valuables, bought herself a flashy coat, had her hair done so that it made her look as plain as possible, but entirely overlooked her shoes and the fact that her nails were freshly manicured."

Drake resumed his gum chewing. He slowly nodded. "Well," he said, "she's in a jam."

"How much of a jam?" Mason asked.

"A forged check for eight hundred and fifty smackers for one thing," Drake said.

"Who cashed the check, Paul?"

"Stylefirst Department Store."

"Some cash and some credit?" Mason asked.

"Credit on a nine-hundred-and-fifty-dollar balance," Drake said. "The department store received the check in the mail, put it through without paying very much attention to it, had it returned marked as a forgery, and got peeved about it. In the meantime, Mae Farr had evidently got wind of what had happened and skipped out."

Mason pushed his chair away from the desk, got to his feet, and started walking the floor, his eyes staring in frowning concentration at the carpet as he walked. "Paul," he flung over his shoulder, "I'm going to ask you a question. I hope the answer to the question is 'no.' I'm afraid it's going to be 'yes.' Was that forged check signed by a man named Wentworth?"

16

"That's right," Drake said. "Penn Wentworth, and it was a lousy forgery."

Mason whirled to stare steadily at the detective. "It was what?" he asked.

"A lousy forgery," Drake repeated.

Mason once more made that characteristic tossing gesture with his right hand. "There you are, Paul," he said. "Another figure in the column which throws the account out of balance. That girl wouldn't have committed a poor forgery. Notice her hands and fingers— long, slender, tapering, artistic, swift and sure about everything they did.

"When she was in here, she was nervous as the devil, but she opened her purse, took out a fresh pack of cigarettes, tore off a corner of the package, took out a cigarette and put it in her mouth, all with smooth, swift grace. That girl can play a piano, can probably paint, and would never, never be guilty of committing a crude forgery."

"Well, she's done it this time," Drake said. "I saw the check. It was payable to Mae Farr in an amount of eight hundred and fifty dollars and was endorsed on the back, 'Pay to the order of Stylefirst Department Store, Mae Farr.' "

"How about her signature on the endorsement?" Mason asked.

"What about it?"

"Did it look all right?"

Drake raised his eyebrows in surprise. "Why the devil wouldn't it look all right?" he asked. "Cripes, Perry, no one is going to forge an eight-hundred-and-fifty-dollar check just to show a department store a good time."

"What," Mason asked, "does Wentworth say?"

"Apparently, Wentworth is very much concerned," Drake said. "Now, here's a funny thing. When that charge account was originally opened, Wentworth guaranteed it."

17

"So he'd be stuck on the account anyway?" Mason asked.

"Yep."

"Then the forgery wouldn't have actually injured him," Mason said. "He was obligated to pay anyway."

"No," Drake said, "if the girl had paid, he wouldn't have had to. His okay was as a guarantor."

"And he's burnt up about the forgery?"

"I'll say. Says that the girl is a base ingrate and that he's going to put her behind bars regardless of what comes of it."

Perry Mason heaved a deep sigh. "Paul," he said, "the whole business is screwy."

Drake glanced across at Della Street. "How's he doing, Della?" he asked. "He's got me interested now. But what about Perry?"

Della smiled. "He's been interested all along," she said, "only he hasn't admitted it to himself until just now."

Mason said, "By gosh, Della, I think you're right." He turned to Drake and said, "Okay, Paul, tell her I'll handle her case. When she comes in, tell her this forgery is a serious business and we should do something to protect her sister. Don't let on that you know the sister business is a stall. I want to spring that on her after she figures she's got away with something—when it'll come out of a clear sky."

"Okay, Perry," Drake said.

"And one more thing," Mason went on. "How about a photostatic copy of that forged check? Do you think you could get me one?"

"Nothing to it," Drake said. "The bank had it photographed. Whenever they turn down payment of a check on the ground that it's forged, they protect themselves by having photostatic copies made. I managed to get one."

"Okay, Paul. Wire the Motor Vehicle Department for a photostatic copy of Mae Farr's driving license. That'll have her signature, among other things. When you get her signature, I'm going to send the photostatic copy of the check and her signature over to a handwriting expert."

"But, my gosh, Perry," Drake protested, "you don't need a handwriting expert to tell that check is a forgery. It's a tracing, and you can see it's a tracing. All the little tremors of the hand which are characteristic of that type of forgery show up plain as day."

Mason said, "I don't want to get an opinion on Wentworth's signature. I want an opinion on the signature of Mae Farr on the endorsement."

The detective's forehead knitted into a perplexed frown.

"Get the picture?" Mason asked. "A department store has a bill of nine hundred-odd dollars against a Mae Farr with a Penn Wentworth as guarantor. They get a check, apparently drawn by Wentworth, payable to Mae Farr, and endorsed over to the department store. They shoot it through in the ordinary course of business. The check is a forgery. It comes back to the department store on the first bounce. They notify Wentworth, and Wentworth goes straight up in the air. Naturally, everyone supposes Mae Farr forged the check because apparently she's the one who stands to profit by the forgery."

"Well?" Drake asked. "You can't get away from that reasoning."

Mason grinned. "Suppose," he observed, "that Mae Farr's signature is also a forgery."

"I don't get you," Drake said.

Mason's grin broadened. "Think it over for a while, Paul. The situation has possibilities."

Mason nodded to Della Street. "Take a letter, Della," he said.

She whipped a shorthand book from the desk drawer and held a fountain pen poised in readiness.

Mason dictated, "To Mr. Penn Wentworth. Drake will give you his address. 'Dear Sir: Miss Sylvia Farr of North Mesa, California, has retained me to locate her sister, Mae Farr, who formerly lived at the Pixley Court Apartments in this city, and to act as her legal representative in any difficulties in which she may be involved.' Paragraph. 'From information contained in some of Mae Farr's letters to her sister, it occurs to me that you may be in a position to give me some information as to the present whereabouts of the party in question. In the event you should, by any chance, be in direct communication with her, please assure her that her sister has made all necessary arrangements for this office to represent her to the extent of its ability.' Paragraph. 'Thanking you in advance for any information you may be able to give, I am very truly yours.' "

As Mason finished dictating, he glanced across at Paul Drake. "Unless I miss my guess," he said, "that letter will get us plenty of action."

3

■

DELLA STREET, entering Perry Mason's office with the morning mail, said, "Your bread on the waters seems to have returned in the form of cake."

"What bread?" Mason asked.

"The letter you sent yesterday to Penn Wentworth."

"Oh, that," Mason said, and grinned. "I'm afraid I'll have to send you to cooking school, Della."

"Why?"

"That bread on the waters," Mason remarked, "isn't going to return in the form of cake. It's going to return in the form of dough."

"Dough?" she asked.

"Exactly," he said. "Mazuma, coin of the realm. How long's he been waiting, Della?"

"About half an hour. He's fit to be tied."

"Bring him in," Mason said.

Penn Wentworth was in his early fifties. He had apparently tried to hide the evidence of those years by devoting a great deal of careful attention to grooming. His clothes were faultlessly pressed. His girth, compared with his chest, the fit of his clothes, and his carriage, indicated that the natural sag of his stomach was held in check by an elastic belt.

His hands were well cared for, the nails carefully manicured. The face, pink and velvety from the ministrations of a barber, was in sharp contrast with the grayish green of his pale eyes. He wore a small, neatly trimmed moustache carefully waxed at the ends.

"Good morning, Mr. Mason," he said.

"Hello," Mason observed casually. "Sit down."

Wentworth accepted the indicated chair. His eyes appraised Mason as the eyes of a skillful bridge player sweep over the cards when he first picks up his hand. "Nice weather," he said.

Mason's face became granite-hard. "Think it'll rain?" he asked.

"No," Wentworth said. "Just a high fog. I received your letter, Mr. Mason."

Mason said, "Personally, I think it's going to rain. What about the letter?"

"I feel that an explanation is due you."

Mason said gravely, "That's fine. I always like to get everything that's due me."

"Don't misunderstand me, Mr. Mason."

"I won't," the lawyer said.

"What I meant was that you have undoubtedly been tricked. A man of your standing, reputation, and ability certainly wouldn't have agreed to represent Mae Farr if he had known all the facts."

"Smoke?" Mason asked.

"Yes. Thank you."

Wentworth's hand came across to the humidor which Mason extended. His fingers picked out a cigarette. He seemed glad of the interruption.

Mason scraped a match into flame, lit the cigarette, tossed the match carelessly into the wastebasket, and said, "Go on."

"It will perhaps come as a surprise to you to learn that Miss Farr is a fugitive from justice," Wentworth said.

"Indeed," Mason observed tonelessly.

"The police hold a warrant for her arrest."

"What's the charge?" Mason asked.

"Forgery."

"Of what?"

"Of a check," Wentworth said indignantly, "a check which constituted a base betrayal of a friendship. The girl is a gold digger, an ingrate, a selfish, scheming—"

"Just a moment," Mason said, pressing a button.

"As I was saying," Wentworth observed, "she—"

Mason held up his hand, palm outward. "Wait just a moment," he said. "I've rung for my secretary."

"Your secretary?"

"Yes. I want her to take down your comments about the moral integrity of my client."

"Look here," Wentworth said in sudden alarm, "you're not going to try to use any of this."

Della Street opened the door from the outer office. Mason said, "Della, I want you to take down Mr. Wentworth's comments about Mae Farr."

Della flashed a glance of calm appraisal at the uncomfortable visitor, then came across to the desk and slipped Mason a note.

The lawyer, unfolding the interoffice memo, read, "Harold Anders waiting in outer office. Wants to see Penn Wentworth about a personal matter which he refuses to disclose. His address is North Mesa, Calif. Said he was told Wentworth was here and said he will wait for Wentworth to come out."

Mason slowly tore up the sheet of folded paper, dropped the pieces into the wastebasket.

22

Wentworth said, "What I was saying was just between us."

"Surely," Mason said, "you wouldn't make such serious charges against a young woman unless you could prove them."

Wentworth said, "Don't try to trap me, Mason. I came here in good faith to warn you about the type of person with whom you're dealing. I don't intend to expose myself to a suit for defamation of character."

"Rather late to think of that now, isn't it?" Mason asked.

"What do you mean?"

Mason turned abruptly to Della. "Send Mr. Anders in," he said. "Tell him Mr. Wentworth will talk with him right here."

Wentworth half rose from his chair. He looked at Mason with eyes that held some measure of suspicion and alarm. "Who," he asked, "is Anders?"

As Della Street slipped quietly through the door to the outer office, Mason said soothingly, "Just a chap who wanted to see you on a personal matter. He's been trying to locate you, heard that you were here, and followed you."

"But I don't know any Anders," Wentworth said, "and I don't think I want to see him. Can't I leave through this exit door, and . . ."

"But you don't understand," Mason said. "He comes from North Mesa. I think he wants to see you about Miss Farr."

Wentworth got to his feet. He had taken two steps when Della opened the door from the outer office and a tall, rawboned man in his early thirties came striding into the room.

"Which one of you is Wentworth?" he asked.

Mason waved his hand in an affable gesture. "The gentleman heading toward the exit door," he said.

Anders strode across the room, moving with a decep-

23

tive swiftness which cut off Wentworth's retreat. "Wentworth," he said, "you're going to talk with me."

Wentworth tried to brush past him. Anders grabbed him by the shoulder of his coat. "You know who I am," he said.

"I've never seen you in my life."

"Well, you know of me."

Wentworth said nothing.

Anders said, "Of all the slimy, contemptible tricks I ever heard of, this business of having Mae arrested takes the cake. A lousy eight hundred and fifty bucks. Here, here's your eight hundred and fifty. I'm making the check good."

He pulled a roll of bills from his pocket and started peeling off twenties. "Come over to the desk where we can count this money. I want a witness, and I want a receipt."

"You can't pay off that check," Wentworth said.

"Why not?"

"Because the entire matter is in the hands of the district attorney. I would be compounding a felony if I accepted this money. Mr. Mason is a lawyer. He can tell you that's right. That's true, isn't it, Mr. Mason?"

"Consulting me professionally?" Mason inquired.

"Oh bosh! I'm merely commenting on what is general information."

"Put your money away, Anders," Mason said. "Sit down. You too, Wentworth. While you're both here, I have something to say to you."

"I have nothing further to say," Wentworth said. "I came here in the utmost good faith, thinking that I could spare you an embarrassing experience, Mason. I didn't come here to be trapped, tricked, or insulted. I suppose that you carefully arranged this meeting with Anders."

Anders' face showed surprise. "What are you talking about?" he asked. "I never heard of the man in my life."

24

Wentworth looked longingly at the door.

"No, you don't," Anders said. "I've been chasing you all over town. We're going to have a showdown right here and now. Try to get out that door, and you'll wish you hadn't."

"You can't restrain me," Wentworth said.

"Probably not," Anders observed grimly, "but I can beat the living hell out of you."

Mason grinned at Della Street, leaned back in his chair, and crossed his ankles on the corner of his desk. "Don't mind me, gentlemen," he said. "Go right ahead."

"What kind of a trap is this?" Wentworth demanded.

"There's no trap at all," Anders said, quivering with indignation. "You've pulled a dirty, stinking trick. I'm here to tell you you can't get away with it. Here's your eight hundred and fifty dollars."

"I refuse to touch it," Wentworth said. "It isn't the money, it's the principle of the thing."

Abruptly, he jumped to his feet. "You try to stop me," he said, "and I'll call the police. I'll sue you for conspiracy, for . . ."

Mason said to Anders, "Let him go, Anders," and then to Wentworth, "I just wanted you to know that I am representing Mae Farr. It may also interest you to know that I've submitted a photostatic copy of that check to a handwriting expert."

Wentworth, with his hand on the doorknob, stopped to stare at Perry Mason.

Mason said, "My guess is that if *your* signature is forged, *so is that of Mae Farr*."

Wentworth said, "It serves me right for trying to do you a good turn. I should have had my lawyer with me."

"Bring him, by all means," Mason invited, "and when you bring him, you might explain the matter of that check to him and ask him for his advice."

"What do you mean?"

"You," Mason said, "have accused Mae Farr of forging that check, acting purely on the assumption that because the check was sent to the Stylefirst Department Store to be credited to her account, she must have been guilty of the forgery. I submit that you haven't any evidence to back that claim, that you can't prove she mailed the check, that you can't prove she wrote it because the evidence of the handwriting expert will be that she didn't, and that, therefore, the check was forged by some third party."

Wentworth hesitated for a moment, then he said cautiously, "Well, of course, if that is true . . ."

"If that's true," Mason said casually, "you have been guilty of defaming the character of Mae Farr. You have made slanderous assertions to the effect that she is a forger and a fugitive from justice. You have made these to the police and to other persons. You have apparently sworn to a complaint charging Miss Farr with a criminal act. . . . Do get your lawyer, Wentworth. I am sure he will advise you to instruct the bank to pay that check. Come in to see me any time. Ring up my secretary for an appointment. Good day."

Wentworth stared at him with consternation showing in his eyes. Then abruptly he jerked the door open and stepped out into the corridor, leaving Harold Anders staring in perplexity at the laywer.

"Sit down, Anders," Mason invited.

Anders walked over to the big leather chair which Wentworth had just vacated and sat down.

"The trouble with me," Mason observed conversationally, "is that I am a natural-born grandstander. My friends call it a flair for the dramatic. My enemies call it four-flushing. That, coupled with a curiosity about people and an interest in anything that looks like a mystery, is always getting me into trouble. What are your bad habits?"

Anders laughed and said, "I lose my temper too easily.

I can't take 'no' for an answer. I'm too much in love with the soil, and I have a hick outlook."

Mason studied him with twinkling eyes. "It sounds somewhat as though the list had been compiled by a young woman who left North Mesa to come to the city," he said.

"It was," Anders admitted.

Mason said, "I've been retained to represent Mae Farr. As nearly as I can find out, her entire trouble is over this forged check with which you seem to be familiar. I don't think we're going to have any further trouble with that."

"But look here," Anders said, "it's a cinch she didn't forge that check. Mae wouldn't do a thing like that, but what I can't understand is, who did it."

"Wentworth did it," Mason said.

"Wentworth?"

"That's right. We probably won't be able to prove it on him, but he's the one who did it or had someone do it for him."

"Good Lord, why?"

Mason said dryly, "It is quite probable that Wentworth is another individual who can't take 'no' for an answer."

Slow comprehension dawned on Anders' face. Abruptly, he placed his hands on the arms of the big chair, pushed himself to his feet, and had taken two quick strides toward the door when Mason's voice arrested him. "Wait a minute, Anders," the lawyer said, his voice kindly yet packed with authority. "I'm running this show. Come back here. I want to talk with you."

Anders hesitated a moment, his face flushed, jaw pushed forward.

"Come on back and sit down," Mason said. "Remember, I'm acting as Miss Farr's lawyer. I don't want anything done which wouldn't be in her best interests."

Slowly Anders came back and sat down. Mason studied

the rugged features, the bronzed skin, the deep tan at the back of the neck. "Rancher?" he asked.

"Uh huh," Anders said.

"What kind of a ranch?"

"Mostly cattle, one patch of alfalfa, some hay."

"Much of a place?" Mason asked.

"Fifteen hundred acres," Anders said proudly.

"All cleared?"

"No, some of it's in brush. A lot of it's hill land. It's all under fence."

"Good," Mason observed.

For several seconds the men sat in silence, Mason calmly regarding the man who sat across from him. Anders, his angry flush subsiding, studied the lawyer with growing approval.

"Known Mae for some little time?" Mason asked.

"Nearly fifteen years."

"Know the family?"

"Yes."

"Mother living?"

"Yes."

"Brothers or sisters?"

"One sister, Sylvia."

"Where is she?" Mason asked.

"She's there in North Mesa, working in a candy store."

"How did you find out Mae was in trouble?"

"Sylvia got worried about her. She hadn't heard from her for some little time, and then one of her letters was returned saying that Mae had moved and left no forwarding address."

"You don't hear from her regularly?" Mason asked.

Anders hesitated a minute, then said shortly, "No."

"You keep in touch with her through Sylvia?"

"That's right," Anders said, in a tone that implied he considered the question none of the lawyer's business. "But this time she called me to say she was in trouble over a forged check for eight hundred and fifty dollars."

"Have you located Miss Farr?"

"No, I haven't. I wanted you— Well, I'm her friend. I want her address."

"I'm sorry," Mason said. "I don't have it."

"But I thought she employed you."

"The young woman who employed me," Mason said, "explained that she was doing it on behalf of Mae Farr. She said that she didn't know where Mae could be reached."

Anders' face showed disappointment.

"However," Mason said, "if you keep on searching, I feel quite certain you'll be able to locate her. When did you leave North Mesa?"

"Two days ago."

"Where is the sister—Sylvia? Is she still in North Mesa, or did she come with you?"

"No, she's still there, holding down a job. The girls support their mother. Mae has contributed most of the money."

"She stopped sending checks a few months ago?" Mason asked.

"No, she didn't. That's why I was trying to find Wentworth. Sylvia received three checks from Wentworth. He said that Mae was working for him and had asked him to send part of her salary direct to Sylvia."

"I see," Mason observed thoughtfully.

"Look here, Mr. Mason. I don't think we should let this thing rest. I think we should—well, do something about Wentworth."

"So do I," Mason agreed.

"Well?" Anders asked.

"I don't like to jump to conclusions when I haven't sufficient evidence to point the way, but it looks very much as though this is about what happened. Wentworth, as I understand it, is something of a gambler. I don't know the exact nature of his business. Apparently, he's rather wealthy. Miss Farr went to work for him. She didn't care

29

particularly about having her friends know where she was working."

Anders said uneasily, striving to keep doubt from his voice, "That bill in the department store, that . . ."

"That undoubtedly means," Mason assured him, "that she was acting as a hostess in some place which Wentworth controlled, or was doing some work for him which necessitated her coming in contact with the public. He insisted that she should be well dressed and probably sent her to the department store with a letter of guarantee. You'll notice that he didn't agree to pay for the merchandise outright, and, in view of the fact that he sent the checks to Sylvia, it's reasonable to suppose that he kept the bulk of Mae's salary, the understanding being that he was to apply part of it toward paying off the bills at the department store and make the remittances to the sister."

"But she said in her letters that she was working for him and . . ."

"Exactly," Mason amended, "but she didn't say just what she was doing. If she was hostess in a nightclub or something of that sort, it's quite possible that Mae didn't want to tell Sylvia about it."

"I see," Anders said, and then, after a moment's thought, his face brightened. "By George," he said, "that would explain the whole thing. Mae was afraid her mother would find out what she was doing. Her mother's rather old-fashioned and straitlaced. She's not well, and Mae was afraid she might worry."

"Exactly," Mason said.

Anders got to his feet. "Well, Mr. Mason, I won't make a nuisance of myself. I know you're a busy man. I'll— Look here, Mr. Mason, I'm at the Fairview Hotel, three-nineteen. If you see Mae, would you tell her that I'm here and want very much to see her?"

"I'll tell her," Mason said. He stood up as Anders came across to shake hands. The two men were much the

30

same build, tall, muscular, and rugged of feature. Anders' bronzed hand gripped Mason's. "I can't begin to tell you how much I appreciate this," he said. "Look here, Mr. Mason, how about your fees? Can I—"

"No," Mason interrupted, "I think Miss Farr would prefer to make all arrangements herself. Don't you?"

"Yes," Anders said, "she would. Please don't tell her I suggested it."

Mason nodded.

"And you'll let me know if you hear anything?"

"I'll tell her where you are."

Anders said, "Gosh, Mr. Mason, I'm certainly glad I met Wentworth here. Otherwise I'd probably have made a fool of myself. Good-bye."

"Good-bye," Mason said.

Anders hesitated a moment uncertainly, then bowed to Della Street, who had sat silently throughout the conversation. "And thank you very much, Miss . . . ?"

"Street," Mason said. "Della Street, my secretary."

"Thank you very much, Miss Street."

Anders walked to the exit door with the long, free stride of a man accustomed to the outdoors.

When the door had closed behind him, Della glanced up at Perry Mason. "Do you believe that story?" she asked.

"What story?"

"The one you told Anders, the explanation for Mae Farr's conduct."

Mason grinned, "Gosh, Della, I don't know. It was the best I could do offhand. Dammit, I wish I didn't get so interested in people and so sympathetic with their problems."

Della Street's eyes were a trifle wistful. She said thoughtfully, "It was a peach of a story."

4

■

MASON, relaxed from a hot shower, clad in thin, silk pajamas and sprawled out in a reclining chair, was immersed in a mystery story. Ominous thunderheads, which had been gathering all afternoon over the high mountains to the north and east, had begun to drift toward the city, and the rumble of distant thunder became increasingly audible as Mason turned the pages of the book.

Abruptly the telephone rang.

Mason, without taking his eyes from the book, stretched out his arm and completed a groping search by closing his fingers around the instrument. He lifted it and said, "Mason speaking. What is it?"

Della Street's voice said, "I think you'd better come down here, Chief."

"Where?"

"My apartment."

"What's wrong?"

"I have a couple of rather excited clients here."

"You've talked with them?"

"Yes."

"And think I'd better come?"

"If you can."

"Okay, Della. Be there in fifteen minutes. Remember, apartment walls are thin. Excited voices always attract attention. Put a muzzle on them until I get there."

She said, "The place is under gag rule right now. I figured you'd want to hear the details firsthand."

"Good girl," Mason said. "I'll be right over."

He telephoned the night man at the garage to have his car waiting, dashed into his clothes, and beat his promised schedule by a minute and five seconds.

In Della Sreeet's apartment he found his secretary clothed for the street, a raincoat over her arm, her hat on, a shorthand notebook and a purse under her arm.

Seated side by side on the davenport across from her, looking very white-faced and big-eyed, were Harold Anders and Mae Farr.

Mason nodded his approval at Della Street's preparedness and said to Anders, "Well, I see you've found her."

Mae Farr said, "You mean that you really did know all along?"

"About you being Mae and not Sylvia?" Mason asked. She nodded.

Mason said casually, "Of course. That was all that interested me in the case in the first place. What's the trouble?"

Anders started to say something. She placed her hand on his forearm and said, "Let me tell him, Hal. Penn Wentworth is dead."

"What happened?" Mason said.

"Someone shot him."

"Where?"

"On his yacht, the *Pennwent*."

"How do you know?" Mason asked.

"I was there."

"Who killed him?"

Her eyes faltered.

"I didn't," Anders said.

"No," she said hastily, "Hal didn't."

"Who did?"

"I don't know."

"How did it happen?"

She said, "I was struggling with him, and someone leaned down through the open skylight in the cabin and shot him."

Mason's eyes narrowed. "You looked up?" he asked.

"Yes."

"See anyone?"

"No. The flash and the shot made me a little goofy, I guess. I didn't see— Well, I could see a shadowy figure. That was all."

Mason, frowning, stared steadily at her.

"You see," she explained hastily, "it was light there in the cabin. This figure was standing against the darkness up above. The skylight was open because it was so airless and—well, I had my hands full. Penn was trying to—trying to—"

"Okay," Mason said. "You don't need to draw me a diagram. What happened?"

"I'm not certain whether it was Penn who said something, but I heard someone say something. I couldn't tell just what the words were, and Penn looked up."

"What was your position?" Mason asked.

"I was twisted around. My hips were on the cushion in one of the seats in the cabin. His knee was in my stomach. His right hand was trying to choke me. I had twisted my shoulders around so I could bite at his wrist and keep him from getting a good hold on my throat. Both of my hands were clawing at his bare arm."

"Bare?" Mason asked.

"Yes."

"Did he have any clothes on?"

"Just his underwear."

"What happened?"

"Someone called something, and I think Wentworth must have looked up at the skylight, and then—then *bang,* it happened."

"Kill him instantly?"

"He rolled off the cushioned seat, doubled up with his hands over his face, and ran aft out of the cabin."

"Then what?" Mason asked.

"I looked up and could see someone moving. I heard steps on the deck. I ran back to the door that goes to the after cabin. I called out to Penn to ask if he was hurt. He didn't answer. I tried to open the door. He must have been lying against it. I couldn't push it open."

"It opened *into* the after cabin?"

"That's right."

"Then what?" Mason asked.

"Then I ran up on deck."

"Where did you meet Anders?"

"On the deck," she said, shifting her eyes quickly.

Mason scowled and glanced at Anders.

Anders said, "Here, let me tell this, Mae."

"By all means," Mason said.

"I distrusted this man, Wentworth. I thought he might know where Mae was or that Mae might try to get in touch with him. I went down to the Yacht Club where he keeps his boat."

"So you found her?"

"Yes. About nine-thirty she drove up to the Yacht Club."

"What happened?" Mason asked.

"She left the car and went aboard, and I . . . well, I . . ."

"Go ahead," Mason said impatiently. "What did you do?"

"I lost my nerve," Anders admitted. "I thought she'd gone aboard voluntarily and—and that perhaps she'd thank me to keep out of her business."

"A wise assumption," Mason said. "Let's have the rest of it."

"Well, I sat there, feeling like a heel, lower than a snake's belly, and—"

"For the love of Mike," Mason interrupted. "I know how you felt. I know the thoughts that were going through your mind. I want facts! We may have to move fast. What happened? Give it to me straight from the shoulder and fast."

"I heard Mae scream," Anders said. "I jumped out of the car and started toward the yacht. She screamed again. The yacht was tied to a float. There's a walk run-

35

ning the length of the float, and then a lot of U-shaped stalls. . . ."

"I know all about that," Mason said. "You don't need to go into those details."

"No, but it's important," Anders insisted. "You see, Mr. Mason, my eyes were blinded by watching the lights on the yacht, and I was running fast—"

"—and he fell in," Mae Farr interposed.

"I fell in," Anders said.

Mason looked from one to the other and said grimly, "The hell you did."

"That's right. I fell in, and it must have been just at that moment when the shot was fired. You see, I didn't know anything about it. It happened while I was in the water.

"You swim?" Mason asked.

"Oh yes. I'm a good swimmer."

"A champion swimmer," Mae Farr amended.

"Well, I've won a few events, no big competition, just interscholastic stuff."

Mason looked at his dry clothes and said, "What happened to your clothes?"

"I changed them," Anders said, "while Mae was telephoning your secretary."

"Where?"

"In the car."

"Carried an extra suit with you in the car?" Mason inquired skeptically.

Anders said, "I was—wearing overalls."

"Don't you see?" Mae Farr explained. "He was trying to shadow Penn, and he thought he needed a disguise. Penn had already seen him, you know. So Hal put on some overalls and one of those round caps that workmen wear, and—"

"And your other clothes were in the car?" Mason interrupted.

Anders nodded.

"Did you have a gun in that car?" Mason asked.

"Yes."

"Where is it now?"

"I— We threw it away."

"Where?"

"Driving back from the Yacht Club."

"When?"

"About thirty or forty minutes ago."

Mason shifted his eyes to Mae Farr. "You called the police?" he asked.

She shook her head.

"Why not?"

"Because no one except Hal knew I was aboard the yacht, and—well, finding Hal there with his clothes all wet, it would have been impossible."

"Why did you go aboard the yacht?" Mason asked.

"I wanted to try and make Penn listen to reason."

"You'd tried before, hadn't you?"

"Yes."

"Get anywhere?"

"No—but you don't understand."

Mason said, "All right then. Go ahead and make me understand."

"Penn," she said, "wanted to— Well, he wanted me."

"I gathered as much," Mason said.

"But he was willing to do anything. You know, he wanted to marry me."

"And you said 'no'?"

She nodded.

"Ever say 'yes'?" Mason asked.

"No," she said, with an indignant shake of her head.

Mason said, "Well, you've made a sweet mess of it now."

"I know," she said, blinking her eyes rapidly.

"Cut it," Mason ordered sternly. "Don't start bawling."

"I'm not going to," she said. "I don't cry. Tears are a confession of weakness, and I *hate* weakness. I *hate* it."

"That vehemently?" Mason asked.

"A lot more than that."

Mason noticed that Anders seemed distinctly uncomfortable.

"Who knew you were going down to the yacht to see Wentworth?" Mason asked.

"No one."

"No one at all?"

"No."

"Where's your car?"

Sudden dismay showed in Mae's eyes. "My God," she said, "we left mine down there. Hal rushed me over to his car and—"

"Your car or one you'd rented?" Mason asked.

"One I'd rented from a drive-yourself agency," Anders said.

Mason's eyes narrowed. "All right," he said, "let's get going. We drive back to that Yacht Club. You go aboard the yacht. Disarray your clothes the way they were during your struggle. . . . How was this struggle? Any bruises?"

"Good Lord, there should be. We fought enough."

"Let's take a look," Mason said.

She hesitated for a moment, glanced at Anders.

Mason said, "Forget it. This is no time to be coy. Go in the bathroom if you have to, but *I* want to see those bruises."

Mae took hold of her skirt on the left side and pulled it up midway on her thigh. "There's one," she said.

Mason nodded. "Any more?"

"I don't know."

"Go in the bathroom with her," Mason said to Della Street. "Take a good look. I want to be damn certain she has bruises."

As the girls went into the bathroom, Mason stared at Harold Anders and said, "Your story stinks."

"It's the truth."

"It stinks just the same," Mason said. "What are you holding back?"

Anders said, "Mae thinks I'm weak. She hates me for it."

"Are you?" Mason asked.

"I don't know. I don't think so."

"What makes her think you're weak?"

"Because I hung around there carrying a gun. She said a real man would have stepped out of the car and grabbed her before she'd gone aboard the yacht, or followed her aboard the yacht, or gone aboard and given Wentworth a damn good beating."

Mason said moodily, "She may be right at that."

The bathroom door opened. Mason had a glimpse of Mae Farr in flesh-colored underwear struggling back into her dress. Through the crack in the door, she saw Mason's eyes on her and said, "Do you want to look, Mr. Mason?"

Mason glanced at Della Street. "Any luck?" he asked.

"Lots," she said. "She's been mauled all right."

"No," Mason said to Mae Farr. "Get your dress on."

Della Street closed the bathroom door. Mason started pacing the floor. When Mae Farr emerged from the bathroom, Mason said, in a low voice, "All right, you two. Anders, you go to your hotel, have a chat with the night clerk, get him to notice the time. Tell him you can't sleep. Stick around the lobby. Mae, you're going back down to that Yacht Club with me. You're going aboard the yacht. After looking the situation over to make damn certain there's nothing that's going to prove you a liar, you start screaming for help. You'll run up on deck with your clothes disarrayed. Scream and keep on screaming until someone notices you. Then you tell your story."

"You mean about coming here and . . ."

"Certainly not," Mason said. "You were struggling with Wentworth. Someone shot him. He ran into the after cabin. You tried to follow. You were half unconscious from

39

the struggle. You tried the door. His body was jammed against it so you couldn't open it. You tried and tried. You don't know how long—it seemed forever. Finally, you succumbed to hysteria and began screaming for help. Think you can do that?"

"Yes, I guess so."

"Well," Mason said, "it's the only way you can get yourself out of the mess. Your car's down there. Your fingerprints are all over the cabin. I don't suppose you thought to wipe your fingerprints off, did you?"

She shook her head.

"Wentworth in his underwear. There are probably fingernail marks on his arm. Your clothes are torn and your body is bruised. The police won't take more than two guesses to figure out what he was doing."

"But why shouldn't I try and get out of it?" she asked. "Why shouldn't I wipe my fingerprints off the knobs, get my car, and . . ."

"Because they'll start looking for the woman in the case, and then start looking for her boyfriend," Mason said. "They'll trace Anders and pin a first-degree murder rap on him. As it is now, they'll only ask for second-degree or manslaughter, and if worst comes to worst, and you can make the story of that struggle sound realistic enough, we can get a justifiable homicide out of it. But you two try to cover the thing up, and here's what'll happen: The D.A. will claim you'd forged a check, that Wentworth was holding it over you, that you went down prepared to offer him almost anything to square the rap."

"They can see," she said, "that I was fighting for my honor."

Mason stared steadily at her. "They can see it," he said ominously, "unless they can prove that you'd already been his mistress, and if they can prove that, God help you."

She stared steadily at the lawyer, her face utterly devoid of expression.

"All right," Mason said, "let's get started. We've wasted too much time already."

"How about me?" Anders asked. "Do I stay at the hotel until—the police come?"

"No," Mason said, "but stay there until I call. I want to look the thing over. I'll telephone you before the police can possibly nab you. Then, probably, the thing for you to do will be to go to another hotel, register under an assumed name, and lie low, pretending that you were planning on taking other steps to get in touch with Mae, and didn't want anyone to know what they were. I'll give you a ring. Come on, Mae. Let's go. Della, I'm playing with dynamite. You can keep out of it if you want to."

"I don't want to," Della Street said, "not if I can possibly help."

"Okay," Mason said. "Come along."

5

■

A FEW SCATTERING drops of rain spattered against the windshield when the car was halfway to the Yacht Club. Behind them, the stars were blotted out by great banks of clouds from which came the flash of lightning, the crash of thunder. By the time they reached the harbor, they had left the thunderstorm behind.

"Which way?" Mason asked the girl at his side.

"Turn right at this next intersection. Now go slow. You have to make another turn within a few hundred feet. It's right along in here. It's just by that fence. There it is. Turn here. There's a place to park cars over on the left."

"Where is your car parked?"

"Right over there."

Mason said, "Wait a minute. Tell me your license number and describe the car."

"It's a Ford convertible," she said. "The license number is WVM five-seven-four."

Mason said, "Sit here for a few minutes."

He switched out the lights, said, "Keep an eye on her, Della," slid out of the car, and walked around the parked automobiles until he spotted the car Mae Farr had described. After a few minutes he came back and said, "Everything's quiet along here. Let's get aboard that yacht and look things over. Della, you'd better stay here."

Della said, "Let me go. You may want to take some notes."

"All right," Mason said. "If you feel that way about it, come along. You show us the way, Mae."

Mae Farr hung back, a trembling hand on Mason's arm. "Gee," she said, "I don't know if I can . . . can face it."

Mason said, in a low voice, "If you haven't nerve enough to make the play, let's not take a crack at it. I have no great desire to stick my neck out. As far as you're concerned, it's the only way you can save your boyfriend. Do you love him that much?"

She said very emphatically, "I don't love him at all. He thinks he loves me. Perhaps he does. I don't know. I put him out of my life when I left North Mesa. I was never cut out to be the wife of a rancher."

Mason looked at her curiously.

She went on to say calmly, "I'm doing this for him because I think I owe him that much. I'd much prefer that he stayed home and minded his own business, but he did what he could to help me."

Mason said quietly, "Do you think he shot Wentworth, Mae?"

42

Mae Farr tightened her grip on Mason's arm. "I don't know," she said. "Sometimes I think— No, he wouldn't lie about it."

"All right," Mason said. "I can't hold your hand through the mess that's going to come next. How about it? Do you want to go through with the thing the way I suggested or telephone the police and give them the whole story?"

"The way you suggested," she said quietly, "but give me a minute to get my breath. I hate to go back in that cabin."

Mason cupped his hand under her elbow. "If you're going to do it, get started. If you're not going to do it, say so."

"I'm going to do it," she said.

Mason nodded to Della Street. The three of them walked from the parking lot down to the long float where a miscellaneous assortment of boats were crowded into U-shaped stalls, a tangle of masts stretching up to where the edges of advancing clouds obscured the starlight.

"That thundershower's catching up with us," Mason said.

No one answered. Their feet sounded on the cross boards of the float. A vagrant breeze, springing up, sent little ripples of water slapping against the sides of the boats.

Mason asked, "Where is this yacht?"

"Down toward the far end," she said.

They walked on. At intervals they passed yachts in which there were lights. From some of them came the sounds of merriment, from one, the tinkle of a guitar. From another, a girl's voice, sharp with indignation, asked someone where he thought he got off, told him he was no gentleman but a four-flusher, a cad, and a cheapskate.

Mason said, "Well, where the deuce is this yacht?"

"It shouldn't be much farther."

"Do you know it when you see it?"

"Of course. I've . . . I've cruised on it quite frequently."

"A big one?"

"Uh huh. Pretty big, about fifty feet."

"Motor and sail or just motor?"

"A motor sailer. It's an old-timer, what Penn called a 'character' boat, but the whole thing is the last word. Lots of electronic equipment and even what they call an Iron-Mike."

"What's an Iron-Mike?" Della asked.

"An automatic steering thing," Mae Farr said. "You switch the thing on, and it's connected in some way with the compass and the steering wheel. You set the course you want the yacht to travel, and it never gets off that course. As soon as it starts to veer, the compass sets an automatic mechanism into action. I don't know the details, but it works perfectly."

Mason said, "Well, there are three boats between here and the end of the landing. Is it one of those three?"

Mae Farr stood stock-still, staring incredulously. "No," she said, "it isn't."

"You mean we've passed it?" Mason asked.

"We couldn't have—but I think we've come too far."

"Okay," Mason said, "let's go back. Keep your mind on what you're doing. Watch for the yacht carefully."

They walked slowly back along the landing until they could once more see the parking lot. Mae Farr said, in a half whisper, "It isn't here."

"All right," Mason said. "Let's find out where it was. Can you remember what boats were next to it?"

"No," she said, "I don't think I can. When I came down, I just walked along here until I saw it."

"Then it wasn't near any of the large yachts?" Mason asked.

"No. I remember it was between two rather small

yachts. Oh, wait a minute. I think one of them was the *Atina*."

Mason said, "Okay, let's look for the *Atina*."

They walked slowly back toward the end of the float, and Mason said, "There's the *Atina* just ahead. There's a vacant space next to it."

Mae Farr stood staring, then turned to Mason. "I remember now," she said, "that it was here. I remember that water barrel near the end of the slip there. She's gone."

Mason's eyes narrowed. "Is there a watchman here?" he asked.

"Yes, he lives in that houseboat. I don't know what they have him for except to answer the telephone and take out messages. I think they lock the place up around midnight. You know, that gate that we drove through. The club members have keys."

Heavy raindrops began to spatter down on the landing and in the water.

Mason said, "All right. That thundershower is going to catch up with us. Get back to your car. I'll drive into town. You drive right behind me. Now, how about this place where Anders tossed the gun? Do you think you can find that place?"

"Yes, I think so. I know about where it was."

"All right," Mason said. "When we come to that place, blink your headlights on and off. We'll stop. I have a flashlight. We'll get out and pick up that gun."

"But what could have happened to the *Pennwent*?" she asked.

"Only one thing," Mason said. "It was moved and probably under its own power."

"Then that means—that someone—would have had to be aboard."

"Exactly," Mason said.

"Who could it have been?"

Mason stared at her with narrowed eyes. "How about

this boyfriend of yours?" he asked. "Does he know anything about engines or yachts?"

"He . . . Yes, I think he does."

"What makes you think so?"

"When he was going through college, he worked one summer up in Alaska on some fishing boats, and I think he's been on at least one cruise from San Francisco to Turtle Bay."

Mason said, "All right. Let's get out of here. We'll talk that over later."

He piloted Mae Farr over to her car, said, "You'd better drive out first and keep the lead until we hit the main boulevard back to town. If anyone stops you, I'll do the talking. After we hit the main boulevard, I'll take the lead. If anything's going to break, it will happen before then. Remember to blink your lights when we come to the place where Anders threw the gun."

"I will," she promised.

"Feel all right? Think you can drive the car?"

"Yes, of course."

"All right. Get going."

The rain was falling more rapidly now, the flashes of lightning were more brilliant, and, at intervals, thunder crashed.

Mason and Della Street climbed back into Mason's car. The lawyer started the motor, switched on the lights, and followed Mae Farr out of the parking place, the windshield wiper swishing back and forth monotonously.

"Think she's lying?" Della asked quietly.

"I don't know," Mason said. "She's a woman. You should know more about it than I do. What do *you* think?"

"I don't know," Della admitted, "but it seems that she's keeping something back."

Mason nodded absently, watching the red glow of the taillight on the machine ahead. "The more I think of it," he said slowly, "the more I'm relieved that I didn't get aboard that yacht."

Della said, "I suppose there's no use pointing out to you that you were taking an awful chance."

"No use whatever," Mason said with a grin. "I have to take chances. When I take on a case, my duty and loyalty are one hundred percent to my client. I do everything in my power to get at the facts, and sometimes I have to cut corners."

"I know," Della said quietly.

Mason glanced at her. "That's no sign that you have to stick *your* neck out," he said.

Apparently Della considered the statement called for no comment.

They drove along in silence for five or six minutes until they reached the boulevard. Then Mason swept on past Mae Farr's car. Della Street asked, "Want me to keep an eye on her headlights?"

"No, I can watch them in the rear-view mirror," Mason said.

The rain was lashing down in torrents. Bolts of lightning zigzagging across the sky illuminated the landscape with weird greenish flashes followed almost instantly by deafening crashes of thunder.

After some fifteen minutes the lights behind Mason blinked on and off. The lawyer pulled his car over to the side of the road and stopped. Mason turned up the collar of his coat against the rain and sloshed back to where Mae Farr's car was standing with idling motor, the windshield wiper clacking back and forth. The headlights showed the falling raindrops, turned them into golden globules.

Mae Farr rolled down the window as Mason came abreast of the car. "I think it was right along in here," she said.

"How positive are you?"

"Pretty positive. I remember that hot-dog stand across

the road behind us. I think we'd passed it just about fifty yards."

Mason looked back at the white building. "It's dark now," he said. "Was there a light in it then?"

"Yes."

"What did he do?" Mason asked. "Stand here and toss the gun, or did he throw it, or did he just open the door of the car and drop it out?"

"No. He got out, stood by the car, held the muzzle of the gun in his hand, and threw it as far as he could throw it."

"Over that fence?"

"Yes."

Mason stared for a moment at the ditch which had already commenced to collect drainage water, and said, "All right. Wait here," walked back to his car, took a flashlight from the glove compartment, climbed over the barbed-wire fence, and started searching through the wet grass, playing the beam of his flashlight around in circles. Whenever other cars approached, he switched out the flashlight and remained motionless until they had passed.

At the end of fifteen minutes, with the batteries in his flashlight running down, Mason climbed back over the fence, fought his way up the slippery embankment at the side of the road, and said to Mae Farr, "It's no use. I can't find it. I'm afraid to hunt any longer."

"I'm quite certain it was right near here."

"Well, we'll know more in the morning."

"What do you want me to do?"

"Where have you been staying?"

"At the address I gave you, the Palmcrest Rooms."

"And we have your telephone number?"

"Yes. I'm awfully sorry, Mr. Mason, that I tried to deceive you. You know, about telling you that I was Sylvia and . . ."

"You'll have a lot of time to make those apologies,"

48

Mason said, "when I'm not standing out in the rain listening to them. I feel a lot more forgiving when cold rainwater isn't dribbling down the back of my neck and when my feet are dry."

"What do you want me to do?"

Mason said, "You have Della Street's telephone number."

"No. We called the office and . . ."

"It's all the same," Mason said. "There's a day number and a night number. The night number is Della Street's apartment. I have an unlisted telephone. She's the only one who has my number. You drive on back to town. Go to the Palmcrest Rooms and go to bed just as though nothing had happened. If anyone drags you out of bed and starts asking questions, don't answer. Don't say a word. Don't admit, don't deny, and don't explain. Insist that you be allowed to call me. I'll do all the talking."

"And if—well, suppose no one does say anything?"

Mason said, "Get up, have breakfast, and get in touch with me in the morning. And for God's sake, keep out of trouble between now and then."

"What do you mean?"

Mason said, "Lay off of Harold Anders. Keep your eyes open and your mouth shut."

She placed her hand on his. "Thank you so much, Mr. Mason," she said. "You don't know how much I appreciate this."

"That also can keep," Mason said. "Good night."

"Good night, Mr. Mason."

The lawyer turned and his wet feet pumped water with every step back to the automobile.

Della opened the car door for him. "Find it?" she asked.

Mason shook his head.

Mae Farr started her car, pulled around them, sounded her horn in two quick blasts by way of farewell, and accelerated down the black ribbon of road.

Della Street opened her purse and took out a small flask of whiskey.

"Where did this come from?" Mason asked.

"Out of my private cellar," Della said. "I figured you might need it. Gosh, Chief, you're soaking wet."

Mason offered her the flask. She shook her head and said, "You need it more that I do, Chief. Drink it down."

Mason tilted the flask to his lips, then handed it back.

"Better take some, Della."

"No, thanks. I'm fine. You certainly were out there long enough."

"I wanted to find that gun," Mason said.

"Think she remembered just where it was?"

"She should have. That hot-dog stand was her landmark."

"It's hard to find anything like that in the dark."

"I know," Mason said, "but I made a pretty thorough search, covered an area seventy-five paces wide by seventy-five long, and what I mean is, I covered it, darn near every inch of it."

"Gosh, you certainly are sopping."

Mason started the car and threw it into gear. "Well," he said, "that's that."

"Make anything of it?" she asked.

"No," he said, "not yet. That whiskey certainly was a lifesaver, Della."

"Where do we go now?"

"To a telephone," Mason said, "and call Hal Anders at the Fairview Hotel."

They drove for miles in silence. The rain became a drizzle, then finally stopped. They found a telephone in an all-night restaurant on the outskirts of the city, and Mason called the Fairview Hotel. "I know it's rather late," he said, "but I'd like to have you ring Mr. Anders. I believe he's in room three-nineteen."

"Was he expecting a call?" the clerk asked.

"It will be quite all right if you ring him," Mason said. "It's a matter of business."

There was an interval of silence, and then the clerk said, "I'm very sorry, but Mr. Anders doesn't answer."

"Perhaps he's in the lobby," Mason said. "You might have him paged."

"No, he isn't here. There's no one in the lobby. I haven't seen Mr. Anders since early this evening."

"You know him?"

"Yes. I didn't think he was in, but I rang his room to make sure."

"Is his key there?"

"No."

"Ring the room again, will you, please? Push down hard on the bell button. He may be asleep."

Again there was an interval of silence. Then the clerk said, "No, sir, he doesn't answer. I've called repeatedly."

Mason said, "Thanks."

He hung up as the clerk started to say, "Any message?"

Mason beckoned Della Street from the automobile. They had a cup of hot coffee at the lunch counter. "Any luck?" she asked.

"None whatever," Mason said. "He wasn't in."

"Wasn't in?"

"No."

"But you told him particularly . . ."

"I know," Mason said grimly. "He wasn't in. I think I'll have some ham and eggs, Della. How about it?"

"Sold," she said.

Mason ordered the ham and eggs. While they were waiting for their order, they sat side by side in silence, sipping coffee. Della Street's eyes were frankly troubled. Mason's profile showed patience, grim determination, and thoughtful concentration.

6

MASON ENTERED his office to find Paul Drake and Della Street in conference.

"Hello, gang," he said, scaling his hat onto the bust of Blackstone by the door. "Why the gloom?"

Drake, looking at the lawyer with eyes that were expressionless, said, "Wentworth is dead."

"The deuce he is," Mason observed cheerfully. "Well, that would seem to simplify matters as far as Mae Farr is concerned."

"Or complicate them," the detective said.

Mason walked over to his desk, sat down on the swivel chair, flashed a swift glance at Della, and received by way of reply a cautious wink.

"Well," Mason said, "let's take a look through the mail. Anything important, Della?"

"Nothing that can't wait."

Mason riffled through the stack of letters and shoved them to one side of his desk. "Well, Paul," he said, "what's the dope? How did Wentworth die?"

"Brain hemorrhage," Drake said.

Mason raised his eyebrows.

"Caused," Drake continued, "by a bullet that went into the right side of the head, struck some of the blood vessels so that there was profuse bleeding, and apparently caused a slow hemorrhage into the substance of the brain, which was the cause of death."

"Death instantaneous?" Mason asked.

"Apparently not."

"Who did it?"

"No one knows."

"When?"

"Sometime last night. They haven't established the exact time."

Mason turned to Della Street so that his face was partially concealed from the detective. "Did you notify our client?" he asked.

"I gave her a ring," Della said. "She wasn't available."

"Where is she?"

"No one knows. She doesn't answer the telephone at her apartment."

"Now that," Mason said slowly, "is *something*."

"You don't know the half of it yet," Della said significantly, with a slight gesture of her head toward Paul Drake.

"Okay, Paul," Mason said, "let's have the other half. You do all the talking for a while, and after I have all the facts I'll do a little thinking."

Drake coiled himself up in the big leather chair and fed three sticks of chewing gum into his mouth. His eyes remained veiled and expressionless. The rapid motion of his jaws as he chewed the gum into a wad furnished the only indication of any nervousness.

"Wentworth," he said, "has a yacht, the *Pennwent*. It's around fifty feet, rather an elaborate affair, with lots of gadgets, including an Iron-Mike. In case you don't know about an Iron-Mike, Perry, it's a device by which the skipper of a boat can link the steering mechanism up with the compass. It enables the ship to be placed on a certain compass course and kept on that course with a very small margin of deviation. The manufacturers claim that a boat is steered by that mechanism a lot more accurately than is possible when there's a man at the wheel."

"Uh huh," Mason said. "I know something about them. Go ahead, Paul."

"About daylight," Drake said, "somewhere off San Diego, the Coast Guard picked this yacht up."

"Why the Coast Guard?" Mason asked.

53

"Well, it's quite a story," Drake said. "A tanker, headed up the coast, had to change course to avert a collision. This yacht ignored signals, seemed to have no lookout aboard, and was running full speed. The skipper of the tanker was considerably peeved. He radioed in a report. A Coast Guard cutter that happened to be cruising in the vicinity picked it up. An hour or so later it saw the yacht plowing along through the water. The cutter signaled it without getting any response, and finally, by a clever piece of navigation, managed to get a man aboard. He found Wentworth's body in the main cabin. Apparently, Wentworth had tried to stop the flow of blood without success. He'd been able to get to the after cabin and returned to the main cabin. He finally keeled over, became unconscious, and died."

"Police find the bullet that did the job?" Mason asked, his voice showing only a casual interest.

"I don't know," Drake said. "I haven't a whole lot of details."

Mason whistled a few bars of a tune, drummed with his fingertips on the edge of his desk. "No one else aboard the yacht, Paul?"

"No."

"Any evidence that anyone had been aboard the yacht?"

"Apparently not. They will, of course, take fingerprints and then they'll know a lot more about it—perhaps."

"Any estimates on how long he'd lived after the shot was fired?" Mason asked.

"Not yet. Anyway, long enough to wander around a little."

"Find the gun?"

"No."

"Where did he keep the yacht?" Mason asked. "Do you know?"

"Yes. He had a berth at the Yacht Club. It would

have taken him about twenty minutes to have cleared the harbor from that berth."

Mason continued to drum with the tips of his fingers on the edge of the desk. Della Street avoided his eyes. Paul Drake, chewing gum rapidly, kept his eyes fastened on the lawyer.

At length Drake asked, "What do I do, Perry? Call the whole thing off or stay on the job?"

"Stay on the job," Mason said.

"Doing what?"

"Getting all the dope you can about that death. Any chance it was suicide?"

"Apparently not," Drake said. "The police don't think so."

"Of course, if he lived long enough to move from cabin to cabin," Mason pointed out, "he could also have tossed the gun overboard."

"There were no powder burns," Drake said, "and the angle of the shot pretty well rules out suicide."

Mason said, "I want to know a lot about this man, Wentworth, Paul. It may be important. I want to know about his friends and associates, his life, his liberties, and his pursuit of what he probably thought was happiness."

"I'm getting quite a bit of that stuff lined up," Drake said. "Part of it was routine that I handled in connection with the job I was on. Some of it is stuff I can get pretty easily, and I figured you'd want it."

"How much of it do you have available now?" Mason asked.

"Not a great deal. He'd been married, and was having some domestic difficulties."

"No divorce?" Mason asked.

"No, that was the rub. His wife is part Mexican—beautiful, olive complexion, streamlined figure, snappy black eyes."

"And a hell of a temper," Mason said.

"And a hell of a temper," Drake agreed. "They separated over a year ago. They couldn't come to terms on a property settlement."

"Why didn't she go to court and let the court give her a slice?" Mason asked.

"Wentworth," Drake interrupted, "was too smart for that racket."

"Lots smarter men than Wentworth have got hooked," Mason said.

"But not such fast workers," Drake said. "Wentworth knew his way around. Apparently, Juanita wanted to marry a man by the name of Eversel, Sidney Eversel. He cuts quite a wide swath. He hangs around with the yachting crowd, has a boat of his own, and takes in all the Catalina cruises and all that jazz. Juanita met him on a club cruise to Catalina. Evidently, it was something of a binge. Juanita became impulsive, and Wentworth objected. After that, Juanita and Wentworth didn't jibe so well. Two months later they separated."

"Had she been seeing Eversel in the meantime?" Mason asked.

Drake shrugged his shoulders and said, "Wentworth employed detectives. Juanita didn't sue for a divorce. You can draw your own conclusions."

"Where was Juanita when Wentworth was shot?" Mason asked.

"I don't know," Drake said. "That's one of the things I'm working on."

"What are the other angles?" Mason asked.

Drake said, "Wentworth got around quite a bit. You know, Perry, a man's home is his castle, but his yacht is his own damn business. Down at the Yacht Club, the party has to get awfully rough before anyone says anything. The only people around are those who have their own boats or their guests. Watchmen of yacht clubs usually go to bed early and don't have good hearing. They have poor eyesight and poorer memories, if you know what I mean."

"You mean Wentworth entertained women aboard his yacht?"

"Scads of them," Drake said. "I have a hunch that there was a party aboard the yacht before it pulled out. Of course, you can't figure that Wentworth was shot and then started putting out to sea. On the other hand, if someone murdered him at sea, did the murderer just step off the yacht into the drink? It's goofy no matter how you look at it. Just on general principles, I'm checking pretty carefully to find out who was aboard the yacht last night. I'm already working on a good lead. A young woman who had been aboard the *Pennwent* several times and was known by sight to some members of the club was down at the Yacht Club last night. One of the members saw her getting out of her car."

"Know who she was?" Mason asked.

"He either doesn't or says he doesn't," Drake said, "but the D.A.'s outfit hasn't really started to work on him yet. When they do, they'll probably get results. I also have some men working on it from another angle."

Mason said, "I'm not so certain that angle is important, Paul."

"I thought you wanted all the dope."

"I do."

"Well, this is part of it."

Mason said, "It might get some innocent girl in an awful jam, Paul."

"Why innocent?" Drake asked.

"Because I don't believe that Wentworth would have taken the yacht out to sea after he'd been shot."

"All right," Drake said, "figure out how someone could have shot him on the high seas and then called a taxicab. Anyway, this girl is in it now right up to her neck. The D.A.'s office will identify her before they get done."

Mason sighed. "Okay, Paul. You can't find out anything sitting in here and gassing."

"I've got five men on the job," Drake said. "Do you want any more?"

"Use your judgment, Paul. I want the facts. I would like to get them in advance of the police if I could."

"You can't," Drake said. "I can pick up crumbs here and there, but the big dish is being served to Homicide. They're working on the case. They have the facilities. And they have the authority."

"Just a minute," Mason said. "How was he dressed when he was found?"

"You mean the color of clothes, or . . ."

"No. Was he fully clothed?"

"Why, yes, I guess so."

Mason said, "Find out, will you, Paul?"

"Okay. I just took it for granted he was dressed because no one said anything to the contrary."

"All right," Mason said. "Get busy and keep me posted."

Drake made no move to get up out of the chair. "You seem to be in a hell of a hurry this morning, Perry."

Mason motioned toward the stack of mail and said, "I have to work for a living. Look at the mail."

"I'm looking at it," Drake said. "I'm also looking at you. This is the first time I ever saw you in such a stew to tackle a pile of correspondence. Let's talk a little sense, Perry. Suppose it was Mae Farr who went aboard that yacht last night?"

Mason raised his eyebrows. "Why pick on her?" he asked.

"Why not?"

"For one reason," Mason said, "she and Wentworth weren't particularly cordial. Wentworth had her arrested on a forgery charge."

"I know," Drake said. "Miss Farr might have figured

she could square that forgery rap if she had a few minutes alone with him."

"There was nothing to square," Mason said. "It was a frame-up."

"I know," Drake said, "but the question is did Mae know?"

"Of course she knew," Mason said. "Her boyfriend was in here when we ripped Wentworth to pieces."

Drake said, "She may have gone down there, Perry."

"What makes you think she did?"

"The description fits."

"Whose description?"

"The man who saw the girl getting out of the car. He knew she was Wentworth's property."

"Wentworth have a brand on her?" Mason asked.

"No, but you know how those yachtsmen are. They stick together. A good-looking, unescorted girl, rubbernecking around at yachts, wouldn't have much difficulty finding some yachtsman who was willing to show her around, but when she belongs to one of the crowd, that's different."

"I don't like that assumption of ownership," Mason said.

"You know what I mean, Perry. A girl who's coming down to call on some particular yachtsman."

Mason said, "Mae Farr is our client."

"I know," Drake rejoined. "The ostrich sticks his head in the sand. You wouldn't want to have any sand in my eyes, would you, Perry?"

Mason said impatiently, "Oh, get the hell out of here, and let me figure this thing, Paul. I'm worried because we can't get in touch with Mae Farr."

Drake said to Della, "Have you tried her boyfriend?"

Della shook her head.

"It might be a good thing to try him," Drake said to Perry Mason.

"It might," Mason agreed.

Drake sighed and began to uncoil himself. He got to

his feet, stretched, yawned, and said, "Have it your own way, Perry. You know what you're doing. I'll keep you posted."

He walked slowly across the office, opened the exit door, and then turned as though about to say something, but he thought better of it and moved silently out into the corridor.

As the door clicked shut, Mason and Della Street exchanged glances.

Mason said, "All right, Della. You're elected. Take your shorthand book."

She picked up her shorthand book from the desk. "Long?" she asked.

"Very short," Mason said.

"All right, I'm ready."

Mason said, "Write 'demand' in caps at the head of the page and then put on a dateline and the words, 'Demand is hereby made that you produce for the inspection of my attorney the original check purported to be signed by Penn Wentworth on which you have refused payment, claiming the same is a forgery. This is a check payable to the undersigned, Mae Farr, and purported to have been endorsed on the back thereof "Pay to the order of Stylefirst Department Store, (signed) Mae Farr." ' "

Della Street's pen flew rapidly over the shorthand notebook.

"Put a blank for a signature on that," Mason said. "Type it out, then put on your hat, and go hunt up Mae Farr."

"You mean go to her apartment?" Della Street asked.

"Go anyplace," Mason said. "Find out all you can. Remember this Demand is your protection, in case anyone asks questions. You're simply looking for her as a part of your duties as my secretary. I want this Demand signed by her so we can serve it on the bank."

"You mean it's just a stall?" she asked.

"Just a stall," he said, "to protect you in case anyone starts checking up."

"How long do I stay on the job?" Della asked.

"Until you find her," Mason said, "or until I give you different instructions. Telephone in every hour or so and let me know what you're doing. Try and get a line on her. Find out if anyone saw her come in or saw her leave. Find out where she keeps her car. Check up on it. In other words, I want everything you can dig up. Feed the facts to me as fast as you get them. If anyone tries to get rough, be wide-eyed and innocent. I dictated this Demand to you and told you to get Miss Farr's signature. You're trying to get it."

Della Street nodded. "On my way," she said, and went out.

At eleven-thirty, Della Street telephoned her first report. "I've located her automobile," she said.

"Where is it?"

"In the garage where she ordinarily keeps it."

"Can you find out what time it came in?"

"Yes, about three o'clock this morning."

"Who drove it in?"

"She did."

"Find anything about her?"

"Not yet."

Mason said, "Do everything you can on that angle, Della. Remember that's one place where we're ahead of the police. I want to get the information before they do."

"I think," she said, "I could work faster if I had one of Paul Drake's men to help me."

"No, that's exactly what I don't want," Mason said. "We can trust Paul, but we can't trust his men. As my secretary, you can be on the job getting a paper signed, and that's all there is to it. If police ask one of Drake's men why he happened to be looking for her, it wouldn't be so good."

"I get you," Della Street said. "What time are you going to lunch?"

"Not until after you telephone again," Mason told her. "Snoop around a little bit and see what you can find."

"Okay, I'll call you back."

Her next call came in less than thirty minutes later. "Someone," she said cautiously, "has taken the lid off the bean pot, and the beans are spilled all over everything."

"What did you find out, Della?"

"Two men," she said, "drove up about nine o'clock this morning and pounded on the door of Mae Farr's apartment until she answered. The men walked right on in and didn't take their hats off. The woman who has the apartment across the court saw that much."

"That," Mason said, "is all she needed to see. Come on back to the office, Della, and we'll go to lunch."

7

PAUL DRAKE was waiting for Mason when the lawyer and Della Street returned from lunch. "Well, Perry," the detective said, "the best I can do is to give you this information about an hour in advance of publication. The newspapers will have it on the street in the early afternoon editions."

"Shoot," Mason said.

"It doesn't look so good for Mae Farr or her boyfriend. I don't know just what lead the police followed, but they followed it right to Mae Farr. I understand the man who saw her leave her car has identified her absolutely."

"Anything else?" Mason asked.

"Yes. They have a lead on the boyfriend."

"Did they find him?"

"I think they had the devil of a time finding him," Drake said. "They picked him up out of town somewhere. The story I get is that they found him up at North Mesa."

"Then what?" Mason asked.

"I understand the girl's sitting tight, but telegraphic advices from the north are that when representatives of the district attorney's office flew up to San Francisco to meet local authorities who had brought Anders down that far, Anders made a fairly complete confession."

"Confession?" Mason asked.

Drake nodded and then said, after a moment, "You're not looking well, Perry."

"What's wrong with me?"

"You don't look right around the eyes. You've been on pretty much of a strain lately. Why don't you take a vacation?"

"Why," Mason asked, "would I want a vacation?"

"I thought it might be a good idea," Drake said. "If I were you, I'd start right away."

"What," Mason asked, "did Anders say?"

"I don't know," Drake admitted, "but it was something pretty hot, I think. The tip that came to the newspapers was that a prominent attorney was going to be implicated."

Mason said, "Bunk. Anders can't implicate anybody."

"It might be well if you were out of the picture for a day or two until I can get all the dope," Drake said. "I can turn the whole thing inside out if I have forty-eight hours."

"To hell with that stuff," Mason said. "Can't you see the field day the police would have if I suddenly took a powder? They'd smear it all over the newspapers that I'd left hurriedly on being advised of Anders' statement."

"Do they," Drake asked, "have anything on you?"

Mason shrugged his shoulders and said, "How do I

know what they have? How did they get Anders to talk?"

"Same old scheme," Drake said. "They told him Mae Farr had confessed to the whole business and was going to take the blame, and he got chivalrous and said it wasn't her fault, and spilled his guts."

Mason said, "Well—" and broke off as the telephone buzzed. Della picked it up, said, "Hello," hesitated a moment, then covered the mouthpiece. She looked up at Perry Mason and said, with no expression whatever in her voice, "Sergeant Holcomb of the Homicide Squad and Carl Runcifer, a deputy district attorney, want to see you at once."

Drake said, "Oh *oh*, those birds get around fast."

Mason jerked his head toward the exit door. "Slip through there, Paul," he said. "Okay, Della, go out and bring them in."

Drake covered the distance across the office with long, easy strides and opened the exit door. A man's voice said, "Hold it. Stay where you are."

Drake stood motionless.

Before Della Street had reached the door to the outer office, it was shoved open by Sergeant Holcomb, who came pushing his way into the office behind a cloud of cigar smoke, his hat tilted back on his head, his eyes hard with hostility.

The man in the corridor called out, "Here he is, Sergeant."

Holcomb strode over to the corridor door, took a look at Drake, and said, "He's just a stooge. Let him go. Come on in, Runcifer."

He held the door open while Carl Runcifer, a tall man in his late thirties with heavy features and gray eyes, walked somewhat sheepishly into the office.

"I thought it was Mason from the description I had," he said.

Mason, behind the desk, said affably, "No apology's

necessary, Runcifer. You're one of the deputies I haven't met. Come on in and sit down."

Runcifer, seeming ill at ease, moved over to the client's chair and sat down.

Mason glanced at Sergeant Holcomb and said, "And how are you, Sergeant? I haven't seen you for a while."

Sergeant Holcomb did not sit down. He stood with his legs spread apart, his hands shoved down into the side pockets of his coat. "Looks as though you've made quite a slip, Mason," he said.

Mason said to Runcifer, "You haven't been in the office long, have you?"

"About three months."

Sergeant Holcomb took the cigar out of his mouth. "Don't try to pull that casual line with me, Mason, because it won't work."

Mason countered, "Don't try to pull that get-you-on-the-defensive line with me, Sergeant, because *it* won't work. If you want to know anything, come out and say so."

"Where's the gun?" Sergeant Holcomb asked.

"What gun?"

"The gun that killed Wentworth."

Mason shrugged his shoulders and said, "You can search me."

"You're damn right I can," Holcomb said grimly.

"Got a warrant?" Mason asked.

"I don't need one."

"It depends somewhat on the viewpoint," Mason observed.

Holcomb came over and sat down on a corner of the desk. "It's one thing," he said, "to act as a lawyer and hide behind this professional-confidence business and this privileged-communication gag. It's another thing to stick your neck out so far that you become an accessory after the fact."

Mason said irritably, "Go ahead. Say it. Get it out of your system."

Runcifer interrupted. "Perhaps, Sergeant, I might ask Mr. Mason a few courteous questions before we make any serious accusations. After all, you know, Mr. Mason is an attorney and . . ."

"Oh hell!" Sergeant Holcomb exclaimed disgustedly, and then, after a moment, said, "Go ahead," and walked across the office to stand in front of the window, deliberately turning his back on Runcifer and Mason.

"I believe you're aware that Penn Wentworth was found dead on his yacht at an early hour this morning?" Runcifer asked.

Mason nodded.

"He had been shot. Circumstances pointed the finger of suspicion at a girl named Mae Farr and a man by the name of Harold Anders. The girl was undoubtedly around last night at the scene of the shooting. Anders admits it, admits that he was in the vicinity of the yacht when the shooting took place. From his story, it probably isn't first-degree murder, but it's undoubtedly a homicide which will have to be cleared up by a jury.

"According to Anders' story, you sent him to his hotel and told him to stay there after Mae Farr had told you all about the shooting. Anders began to think things over and decided that he wanted to consult his own attorney, a friend of long standing who has an office in the county seat where Anders lives. He went down to the airport, chartered a plane, and flew north. He stated all of the facts to this attorney, who advised him to get in touch with the police without delay and make a clean breast of everything. The attorney seemed to—"

"Oh hell!" Sergeant Holcomb interrupted, spinning around from the window. "Why mince words? The attorney said that Mason had given Anders the worst possible advice that a lawyer could give a man."

Mason said, "That's nice."

Sergeant Holcomb went on, "I always told you, Mason, that someday you were going to come a cropper. This is it."

Mason said, "All right, let's quit the schoolboy grandstand stuff and get down to brass tacks. I know you're a smart detective. You should be promoted to a captaincy. You've predicted my downfall for a long time. Anders' lawyer says I gave Anders bum advice. All right, what if he did? I don't care. Anders goes ahead and has kittens. Just because this lawyer gave him the kind of advice you want, you think he's right and I'm wrong. What do *you* want?"

Sergeant Holcomb said, "We want that gun."

"What gun?"

"The gun that killed Penn Wentworth."

"I haven't got it."

"That's what you say."

Mason's face darkened. His eyes narrowed slightly. "That," he announced with cold finality, "is what I say."

"Okay," Sergeant Holcomb said. "We wanted to give you an out. If we have to do it the hard way, we can do it the hard way."

"Go ahead," Mason said, "do it the hard way."

Sergeant Holcomb said, "Just a minute. You stay here with him, Runcifer," and strode across the floor, jerked open the door to the outer office, walked out to the reception room, picked up a small handbag, and returned.

Mason watched him calmly while he opened the handbag, reached inside, then stood for a moment as though setting the stage for a dramatic act.

"Go ahead," Mason said, "pull out the rabbit."

Sergeant Holcomb jerked out a pair of shoes. "Look at these," he said. "Tell me if they're yours, and remember that anything you say will be used against you."

Mason looked at the muddy shoes, reached out, took one, examined it, and asked, "Where did you get these shoes?"

Holcomb said, "Don't think you're going to pull that kind of an act, Mason. I got them with a search warrant."

"Who the hell gave you a warrant to search my apartment?"

"A judge," Sergeant Holcomb said, "and that's not answering the question, Mason. Are those your shoes?"

"Of course they're my shoes. You got them in my apartment, didn't you?"

"Were you wearing them last night?"

"I don't remember."

"The hell you don't."

Mason said, "You're asking the questions. I'm answering them. Never mind the comments. You might get into trouble."

Sergeant Holcomb said, "Don't try bluffing me because it won't work. If I drag you down to headquarters and book you on the charge of being an accessory after the fact, you'll sing a different tune."

"Not to any music you can play," Mason said.

Runcifer said placatingly, "Now, let's not lose our tempers, Mr. Mason. You must appreciate that the evidence is incriminating, to say the least. You must also realize that the minute we take any action, the newspapers will give you publicity which will be highly disadvantageous. Now we are here for the purpose of eliciting information in a courteous manner."

"Why don't you follow your charted course then?" Mason asked.

Runcifer said meaningly to Sergeant Holcomb, "I think we will. Sergeant, if you'll pardon me, I'll do the questioning."

Sergeant Holcomb shrugged his shoulders and turned away contemptuously.

Runcifer said, "Mr. Mason, I am going to be frank with you. Anders has made a complete statement. He said that Miss Farr boarded the *Pennwent*, that he heard her scream and heard sounds of a struggle. He rushed to her rescue. In running across the float, he missed his footing and fell into the water. As nearly as he can judge, the shooting took place while he was in the water because he insists that he did not hear the sound of the revolver shot although he had heard Miss Farr's cries for help quite plainly. Upon boarding the yacht, he ran to the open skylight and looked down into the main cabin. Miss Farr was arranging her clothes, which apparently had been badly disarrayed. She ran up on deck. Upon seeing him aboard the yacht, she became greatly confused and embarrassed, asked him what he was doing there, and when he told her that he came in response to her cries, asked him if he had a weapon with him. Upon being assured that he had, she rushed him off the yacht in the greatest haste.

"Later on, and as they were traveling toward the city in his car, she told him that Wentworth had been shot and that she wanted to rush him off the yacht because she was afraid that persons from neighboring boats would be attracted by the shot and that Anders would be accused of the shooting. Anders thereupon, fearing that such might be the case, decided to get rid of his gun. He stopped the car near a hot-dog stand which he describes perfectly and threw the gun off to the side of the road across the fence which borders the highway. Then they drove to town.

"Thereafter, Anders tells a story which I find it difficult to believe. He claims that—"

Sergeant Holcomb interrupted. "Are you going to tell him every single fact we have in our possession?"

"Absolutely," Runcifer said, his tone reflecting the obstinacy of a man who lives in a world of books, who has acquired his knowledge from abstract study and looks upon the events taking place about him from an academic viewpoint.

"Show 'im all the trump cards you hold before he plays

his," Sergeant Holcomb said, "and he'll know which ace to trump."

"I think this is the only ethical way to handle the matter, Sergeant," Rucifer said with cold finality. "Your methods resulted only in an argument which brought us no additional information and was personally distasteful to me."

Sergeant Holcomb said, "Nuts."

Mason said to Runcifer, "You were saying?"

"Let's see," Runcifer said, frowning. "Exactly what *was* I saying? Oh yes, about what Anders told us took place when he returned to the city. He said that he consulted the telephone directory to see if you had a resident telephone. He found there were two numbers for the office, one a day number, the other a night number. He called the night number, and your secretary, Miss Street, answered. He tried to tell her what had happened over the telephone, and she instructed him to come with Miss Farr to her apartment at once."

Runcifer placed the tips of his fingers together and concentrated his gaze upon them, apparently more concerned lest his summing up of the case should miss some significant detail than in the reactions of Perry Mason.

Sergeant Holcomb stood glowering at the deputy district attorney, apparently of half a mind to step in and assume charge but hesitating because of orders to act under Runcifer's direction.

"Now then," Runcifer went on, in calm, academic tones, "comes the part of the story which seems utterly incredible to me. I cannot understand your actions in the matter, Mr. Mason. However, I will first outline what Anders said. He claimed that Miss Street called you, that you came to her apartment, that you advised both of them to refrain from notifying the authorities, and that you yourself accompanied Miss Farr to the yacht harbor for the purpose of finding some way of keeping her name from being brought into the case.

70

"Anders swears that the *Pennwent* was moored at the float when he left. As you know, the yacht was subsequently found cruising off San Diego, steering a course which would have taken it into the Mexican coast in the vicinity of Ensenada. The body of Penn Wentworth was found fully clothed. Nevertheless, Anders states that Miss Farr insisted that during the struggle with her, he was clad only in his underwear.

"Now then, Mr. Mason—oh yes, one thing more. The police officers naturally wished to check Anders' story. They went to the place where he said he had thrown the gun. He was in the car and indicated the exact spot. You'll remember that there was a thundershower last night, Mr. Mason, and the officers were surprised to discover that someone had made a very thorough search of the ground where Anders had thrown the gun. The footsteps were quite plainly evident in the soft mud which covered much of the field.

"The officers made plaster casts of those footprints, and your shoes make identical marks. Now then, Mr. Mason, there is no other conclusion which seems logical other than that you went to the Yacht Club, that you and Miss Farr, and perhaps your secretary, Miss Street, boarded the *Pennwent*, that you found Penn Wentworth dead, that you desired to keep Miss Farr's name out of the case and to protect her good name in the event she should be dragged into it. Therefore, you placed clothes on Wentworth's body, started the yacht, took it out to the headland, set the automatic steering mechanism on a course to Ensenada, and then left the yacht."

"That's very interesting," Mason said. "How did we leave?"

"Probably by having some other boat come alongside."

"Then what?" Mason asked.

"Then you returned to search for the gun, found it, and removed it."

71

"All this," Mason asked, "is predicated on Anders' story?"

"His confession."

"What did he confess to?"

"Being aboard the yacht, armed and, as he admitted, looking for trouble."

"That's not much of a crime," Mason said. "What did he do?"

"According to his story, he didn't do anything."

"And all that you have against me," Mason said, "is that he told you I left for the Yacht Club with Miss Farr, and he surmised that I had done this and that. Is that right?"

"His surmises are quite reasonable."

Mason said, "Well, I'm sorry I can't help you. I didn't go aboard the *Pennwent*. I didn't dress the corpse. I didn't have anything to do with it. I don't know who did."

"You knew that the dead body of Penn Wentworth was aboard that yacht, Mr. Mason?"

"No."

"You didn't? Why, Anders insists that Miss Farr told you."

"As far as the conversation which occurred between my client and myself is concerned," Mason said, "it's confidential. I have no right to repeat any statements which she made to me or any advice which I gave to her. Therefore, it's out. You can't inquire into it here. You can't inquire into it before a grand jury, and you can't inquire into it in court."

"Subject to certain specific qualifications, that," Runcifer admitted, "would seem to be correct. However, the law of privileged communications is subject to certain well-defined exceptions."

"All right," Mason said. "I'll advance the law. You advance the exceptions. I'm telling you you can't question me concerning the advice I gave a client.

72

"Now then, we come to the rest of it—a claim by Anders that I went to the Yacht Club and he thinks I must have done certain things while there."

"His deductions are most logical," Runcifer insisted.

Mason said, "You'll pardon me if I fail to agree with you."

"What is your explanation?" Runcifer asked.

"I have none."

"Well, I'll put it this way, Mr. Mason. Wherein do you find any departure from logic in Anders' statement?"

Mason said, "That's something I'll argue in front of a jury."

"But look here, Mr. Mason, you were in that field walking around looking for a gun."

"What if I was?"

"You had no right to do that. You should have reported the crime to the officers."

"How did I know there was a crime?"

"You had been advised of the shooting."

Mason said, "Let me ask you a question. Why did you go and look for the gun?"

"We wanted to check up on Anders' story."

"In other words, you thought that it was open to some doubt?"

"Well, it was rather unusual. We thought perhaps he was keeping something back."

"All right," Mason said. "Suppose I say I also felt his story was open to some doubt and decided to confirm it?"

"The gun constituted a complete confirmation."

"What gun?" Mason asked.

"The gun that was there."

"What," Mason asked, "makes you feel that a gun was there?"

Runcifer said somewhat irritably, "Mr. Mason, I didn't come here to bandy words with you. You know perfectly well that the gun was there."

"You looked for a gun this morning?" Mason asked.

"Yes."

"Why?"

"We wanted to check on Anders' story, I tell you."

"In other words," Mason said, "you went out to look because you weren't certain that a gun was there. I should certainly have the same privilege."

Runcifer said, "I don't think that's a fair answer, Mr. Mason. It was the duty of the officers to search for that gun in order to find it and preserve it as a part of the evidence."

Mason said, "So far you've talked about Anders. Why don't you give me the benefit of the story that Miss Farr told?"

"Unfortunately," Runcifer said, "Miss Farr refuses to make any statement whatever. That, I consider, is very much opposed to her best interests."

"You told her about Anders' statement?"

"Naturally," Runcifer said. "We—"

"For God's sake," Sergeant Holcomb interrupted, "we came up here to get information, not to hand this bird everything we know on a silver platter."

Runcifer said, "That will do, Sergeant."

Sergeant Holcomb took two indignant strides toward the exit door of the office, then checked himself and stood with flushed countenance and angry eyes.

Runcifer said, "I don't think your attitude shows a desire to cooperate, Mr. Mason. I have been perfectly fair and frank with you. Because you are an attorney, I don't want to have you placed under arrest without giving you an opportunity to explain."

Mason said, "I appreciate your sincerity and your motives, Runcifer. However, you have nothing to say about it. You're acting under orders. You don't determine the policy of your office. You came here with certain specific instructions. Those instructions were given to you for a purpose. Your office isn't as considerate as you are. If there'd been any grounds on which they could have arrested me, they'd have done so. However, they can't do it. All Anders knows is that I suggested to Miss Farr that we should go to the yacht harbor. I had a right to do that in order to verify her story. That much you will certainly grant.

"As for all the cock-and-bull yarn about dressing the corpse and putting the yacht out to sea, your office has one thing and one thing alone on which to act—the cock-eyed guess of a man who tells a rather remarkable story, namely, that he had been watching Wentworth's yacht, lying in wait with a gun in his pocket; that the girl he loved boarded Wentworth's yacht; that he claims he heard sounds of a struggle taking place, started to run aboard the yacht, and fell into the drink; that at the exact moment when his ears were submerged under water, and his sight of the yacht had been blotted out by a cross section of the Pacific Ocean, some obliging individual stepped aboard the yacht, shot Wentworth, and then withdrew; that Anders, climbing from the water to the float, completed his journey to Wentworth's yacht only to find that the woman he loved was straightening her disarrayed clothing.

"That story, gentlemen, is worse than lousy. It stinks. If you think any jury is going to believe that story, you're crazy as hell. And because that story is so cock-eyed, the district attorney's office and the police aren't quite ready to crack down on me as an accessory after the fact, but they did have enough information to send you and Holcomb up here to ask me for a statement, the idea being that I might be unwise enough to say something which would furnish something by way of corroboration."

"We have those shoes for corroboration," Holcomb said. "That's all the evidence we need."

"The most you can claim for the shoes," Mason said, "is that they prove I was walking around in a field."

"You found the gun," Runcifer charged, "and concealed it."

"Where did I conceal it?"

"We don't know."

"In that event," Mason said, "you'd better get some more evidence before you make any statement of accusation."

Runcifer stared thoughtfully at Mason for several seconds, then he once more regarded his spread-out fingertips. At length he looked up at Sergeant Holcomb. "Any questions, Sergeant?" he asked.

"Questions?" Sergeant Holcomb said in disgust. "You've told him everything you know now, and he's told you nothing he knows. Questions, hell!"

Runcifer said, "I find your attitude insubordinate rather than helpful, Sergeant."

Sergeant Holcomb made some half-strangled, half-articulate reply. "Let's go," he said.

Runcifer got to his feet.

Sergeant Holcomb angrily threw the shoes into the bag, locked it, and strode toward the exit door.

Runcifer followed him, turned at the door, bowed, and said, very precisely, "Good afternoon, Mr. Mason."

Mason, his eyes twinkling, said, "So long, Runcifer."

8

■

MASON RANG for Della Street and when she entered the office said to her, "Della, use our regular office forms. Prepare a writ of *habeas corpus* for Mae Farr. I'm going to make them either file a charge against her or turn her loose."

She studied the granite-hard lines of his countenance with solicitous eyes. "How was it?" she asked.

He shrugged his shoulders.

"What did they do?"

"Not much," Mason said. "It could have been a lot worse. Evidently, Holcomb was under orders to let the D.A.'s office run the show."

"And how did they run it?"

"Their timing was bad," Mason said, "but Runcifer was a gentleman. I don't think he has had much experience as a trial lawyer. He wanted to be certain he'd covered every single detail about which they wanted to question me."

"What did Sergeant Holcomb do?"

"Tried to get rough," Mason said, "found he couldn't get away with it, and turned sullen."

She said, "Paul Drake telephoned that he had some important information and wanted to come in as soon as the coast was clear."

"Okay. Tell him the coast is clear. Get out that application for a writ of *habeas corpus* and ride herd on that outer office. I don't want to see any routine clients, don't want to think about any routine business."

She nodded. "Follow the same procedure as in that Smith case?" she asked.

"Yes. Use the files in that case for form. You can check them over and get the typists started doing the work. I want it right away."

With self-effacing efficiency, Della glided through the door to the outer office. A few minutes later Paul Drake knocked on the corridor door and the lawyer let him in.

"How was it, Perry?" Drake asked.

"Not so bad," Mason said.

"What did they want?"

"The man from the district attorney's office wanted facts," Mason said. "Sergeant Holcomb wanted me."

"Didn't get you, did he?"

"Not yet. What's new?"

77

Drake said, "A lot of things. Here's the latest paper."

"What's in it?"

"The usual hooey and statements that by throwing out a dragnet, police were able to apprehend Anders in a northern city where he had fled, that he's made a partial confession, that as a result of that confession, police are investigating the activities of one of the best-known criminal attorneys in the city, that police are searching for the gun with which they feel the murder may have been committed, that Anders admits having a gun which he threw away. Police were rushed to the scene where they found that virtually every inch of the territory had been covered by a man who made a search sometime after the rain started last night."

"What's the photograph?"

"Sergeant Holcomb holding up a pair of shoes and showing how they fit the plaster-of-paris casts made of the footprints that were found in the soft soil."

"Say where he got the shoes?" Mason asked.

"No, that's one of the things on which the paper reports the officers are working, but are not as yet ready to divulge any information because of the sensational conclusions which may be drawn when the evidence is finally put together. . . . Are those your shoes, Perry?"

"Yes."

Drake said, "That looks rather bad, doesn't it?"

Mason brushed the question aside with a quick gesture of his hand. "Never mind the postmortems," he said. "Give me the facts. What's that other picture?"

"Photograph of the field where the police think you found the gun."

"Let me see it," Mason said.

He took the newspaper, folded it over, and studied the newspaper reproduction of a photograph showing a field alongside the highway.

"Line of high tension poles running along the right of way," Mason said musingly, "barbed-wire fence, concrete pipe lines for irrigation—not much opportunity to conceal a gun there, Paul, just clumps of grass and weeds. Why don't they cultivate that ground if it's under irrigation?"

"It's tied up in litigation," Drake said.

"What else, Paul?"

"Quite a bit of stuff—a whole mess of dope on the tastes and habits of Wentworth."

"Yachting his hobby?" Mason asked.

"Yachting, women, and coin collecting," Drake said.

"Why the coins?"

"You can search me. Coins, boats and horses, wine and women, that represented Wentworth's life."

"What did he do for a living?" Mason asked.

Drake grinned and said, "I think that's going to be a sore subject with the police. Evidently he was a book-maker. He had a partner by the name of Marley—Frank Marley."

Mason said, "I've heard of him. Wasn't he arrested a while back?"

"Two or three times," Drake said.

"What happened to the charges?"

"Postponed, transferred, continued, and dismissed."

"A payoff?"

Drake said, "I'm not saying anything. Perhaps you can read my mind."

"I'm reading it," Mason said, and grinned. "How about Marley? Can we drag him in?"

"I have an idea we can," Drake said. "Incidentally, Marley also has a boat. He went in for fast stuff, an express cruiser with powerful motors, twin screws, mahogany finish—nothing you'd want to be out in a heavy sea in, but something that would scoot over to Catalina and back in nothing flat."

"Where was he last night?"

"Apparently in a hospital. He was scheduled to have an operation this morning—nothing serious. He'd had a

79

couple of attacks of appendicitis, and the doctor told him to have it out when he could spare a few days from his business. He reported to the doctor yesterday and went to the hospital yesterday afternoon."

"Did he have the operation?" Mason asked.

"No. There was nothing particularly urgent about it. When he heard of Wentworth's death, he called off the operation, claims he can't afford to be laid up right now. There's too much business to be handled."

Mason said, "Not that it means anything, but just for the purpose of keeping the records straight, that hospital business doesn't mean a damn thing."

"I know," Drake said. "I've checked on it, however. He had a private room. A special nurse was to come today after the operation, but he was on general last night. Directions called for him to have a capsule of sodium amytal."

"Did he get it?"

"Yes. The nurse gave it to him."

"Would that make him stay put?" Mason asked.

"Yes, I think it would," Drake said. "And the floor nurse looked in on him three or four times during the night."

"Does it show on his chart when she looked in on him?"

"No, but the nurse says it was at least once before midnight, a couple of times after midnight, and once this morning. The special came on duty at eight o'clock. He was to have been operated on at ten."

"Did they tell him about Wentworth?"

"They weren't going to, but he insisted on talking with Wentworth over the telephone before he went under the anesthetic, said he had some last-minute instructions to give and wanted to verify certain matters. They tried to keep it from him but couldn't."

"How about Wentworth's wife?" Mason asked.

"She was down in San Diego. It looks as though Wentworth had an appointment with her for this morning."

"Where?"

"At San Diego."

"And the wife's boyfriend?"

"I don't know, yet. But he has a yacht."

"Where is it moored?"

"Outer yacht harbor, just inside the breakwater."

Mason and the detective exchanged glances.

"Better check him pretty carefully," Mason said.

"I'm doing that. He's quite a sportsman, polo, yachting, and airplanes."

"Airplanes?"

"Yes. He has an amphibian he plays around with."

"Where does he keep it?"

"In a hangar on his estate."

"And that's where?"

"On a rugged promontory overlooking the ocean about ten miles from his yacht mooring."

"Can you find out if the plane has been doing any traveling lately?"

Drake said, "I'm going to try to get a look at the log of the plane."

"How about traveling? That wouldn't be in the log."

Drake shook his head and said, "Barring accident, we can't find out about that."

Mason drummed with the tips of his fingers. "Can you get in the estate, Paul?" he asked.

"It's difficult," Drake said, "but I think I have an operative who could do the job."

Mason said, "There was rain last night, Paul. It came down pretty heavy for a while. If an airplane taxied off a dirt field, it would leave tracks, particularly if it was a little slow on the takeoff."

Drake said, "I get you, Perry."

"How about servants? Can you find out if they might have heard the sound of the motor?"

Drake said, "I could tell you the answer to that in advance, Perry. It's 'no.' "

"How come?"

"There wasn't a servant on the place last night. Eversel gave them all a night off and had the chauffer put a car at their disposal."

Mason raised his eyebrows.

"That's what I thought, too," Drake said, "but it turns out it's not particularly unusual. Eversel has a hard time keeping servants. The estate is isolated. There are no picture shows, beauty shops, or any sort of amusement facilities available. Naturally, you can't expect servants to stay on a job like that seven days a week, fifty-two weeks a year. When they have time off, Eversel has to provide them with transportation if they're going to leave the estate. So he frequently sends them out on a skylarking expedition, especially when he doesn't expect to be home."

"I see," Mason said, his voice casual enough, but his eyes narrowed into thoughtful slits.

"The bullet," Drake went on, "was fired downward, apparently through the skylight or when Wentworth was leaning forward. Probably the shot was fired through the skylight. The windows of that skylight roll back. They're controlled from the inside. In warm weather, while the ship was moored or cruising through calm waters, Wentworth would roll the windows back and get ventilation through the opening."

"It was warm last night," Mason said.

"There's no question but what the glass was rolled back when Anders went aboard," Drake said. "Anders admits that in his statement to the police. He claims that's the reason he could hear Miss Farr pleading with Wentworth and struggling."

"Anyone else hear any screams?" Mason asked.

"No. Apparently, the screams weren't particularly loud. People on yachts don't listen for those things anyway.

Some pretty wild parties go on at times. Most of the time the screams that come from a yacht are referred to as 'the squeals of synthetic virtue.' I'm getting a file of photographs taken by one of the newspapermen, showing the interior of the cabin just after the yacht was brought into the harbor. Incidentally, Perry, Wentworth was probably dead before the rain started."

"How come?"

"He hadn't closed the skylight. He would have . . ."

Della Street slipped quietly through the door from the outer office and came over to Mason's desk. She slid a folded paper across to him. He unfolded the paper and read, "Frank Marley, partner of Wentworth, in the office. Wants to see you at once on an urgent matter."

Mason thought for a moment, then slid the memo across to Drake.

The detective read it and said, "Oh, oh."

"Send him in, Della," Mason said.

The men waited in silence until Della Street escorted Marley into the office and quietly withdrew, closing the door behind her.

Marley, a small-boned, dark, thin man in his late thirties, kept his face without expression as he stood still, glancing from Mason to Paul Drake.

"Come over and have a chair," Mason invited. "I'm Mason. This is Paul Drake, who handles my investigations."

Marley's large, dark eyes, the sheen and color of ripe olives, moved from one man to the other. He smiled, then came forward and extended a hand to Mason. "Very pleased to meet you, Counselor," he said.

Mason's big hand closed over the small, tapering fingers, received in return a grip of surprising strength. Then the huge diamond in Marley's tie flashed as he turned to shake hands with the detective.

His hand dropped to his pocket and took out a cigarette case. A diamond on his ring finger made a glittering streak of light as he conveyed the cigarette to his lips. "I only have a few minutes, Mr. Mason," he said significantly.

"Go right ahead."

Marley smiled. His eyes were without expression. In a low, well-modulated voice, he said, "My information is very confidential."

Drake glanced at Mason, raising his eyebrows. The lawyer nodded, and Drake said, "Okay, Perry. See you later." He studied Marley for a long moment, then he said, "Glad I met you, Marley. Probably see you again."

Marley said nothing.

When he had gone, Mason said, "Well?"

Marley said, "Too bad about Penn."

Mason nodded.

"However," Marley went on, "I'm a man of the world, and I take it, Mr. Mason, that you're a businessman."

Again Mason nodded. "Better sit down."

Marley eased one hip over on the arm of the chair which Drake had just vacated. "You're representing Mae Farr?" he asked.

Mason nodded.

"A nice girl, Mae."

"Know her?"

"Yes. Penn carried a torch for her. I was close to Penn. Sometimes we'd cruise on his yacht, sometimes on mine. It depended on the weather. My boat performs best on a smooth sea. Penn had an all-weather yacht."

Mason nodded.

"Mae's an independent kid," Marley said, almost musingly.

"Any idea who killed him?" Mason asked abruptly.

Frank Marley's dark eyes bored steadily through the light blue haze of cigarette smoke which framed his features. "Yes," he said.

"Who?" Mason asked.

"Suppose I tell you a story first."

"It's your show," Mason said. "Go ahead and run it."

Marley said, "I want something."

"You don't look exactly like a philanthropist," Mason observed.

"What I want means a lot to me and not much to you."

"Go ahead," Mason urged.

"I always figured you were the best mouthpiece in the business. I made up my mind that if I ever got in a jam, I'd come to you."

Mason's acknowledgment was less than a bow, almost a nod.

"I'm apt to be in a jam on this thing."

"How come?"

"Penn was never divorced. He and his wife could never agree on a property settlement. She tried to wear him down. He wouldn't give her a divorce, and she wouldn't give him one. Neither one of them could have had a divorce without the other's consent. It would have resulted in a lot of mudslinging, and a judge would have kicked them both out of court."

"They didn't get along?" Mason asked.

"At first they did. Afterwards, it was just like two cats tied by the tails and thrown over a clothesline."

Mason said, "I suppose that was after you started playing around with her."

Marley's face didn't exactly change expression. It merely stiffened as though he had frozen his facial muscles into immobility at the impact of Mason's remark. After a long moment, he puffed calmly on his cigarette and said, with equal calmness, "What gave you that idea, Mason?"

"Just a shot in the dark," Mason said.

"Don't make them," Marley warned. "I don't like them."

Mason ostentatiously pulled a sheet of paper toward himself, and scribbled a rapid note on it.

"What's that?" Marley asked suspiciously.

"Just making a note to have my detective look up that angle of the case."

"You," Marley announced, "are hard to get along with."

"Not for those who shoot square with me," Mason said. "When a man sits on the other side of the desk and starts trading horses, I trade horses."

"Better wait until you hear the horse trade I have lined up," Marley said, "before you start getting rough."

"I've been waiting ever since you came in," Mason reminded him.

"As I was saying," Marley said, "I think you're a swell mouthpiece. I'd rather have you in my corner than in the other guy's corner. Juanita is still Wentworth's wife. I don't think Penn left a will. She'll have the job of winding up the estate. As the surviving partner, I'll have to account to her for partnership business."

"Well?" Mason asked.

"It's going to put me in a spot," Marley said.

"Why?"

"There were things that Penn knew all about," Marley said, "which wouldn't look so well in black and white. I did certain things. I asked Penn about them before I did them. He gave me his okay. It was all word of mouth, nothing in writing. Naturally, I didn't think he was going to get bumped off."

"So?" Mason asked.

"So I want you to be in my corner."

"For what?" Mason asked. "The preliminary fight or the main event?"

"Just a preliminary," Marley made haste to assure him. "There isn't any main event as far as I'm concerned. I want you to represent me in straightening out the affairs of the partnership."

"That all?"

"That's all."

"How much," Mason asked, "were you prepared to pay?"

Marley said hastily, "Before we start talking about that, I'll tell you some more about the horse I have to trade."

"What about it?"

Marley said, "I don't have too much use for the cops. I've been in business too long. I'm sorry Penn got croaked. Being sorry can't help him any. He's gone. I'm left. I have to look out for myself. All right, here's the proposition: Mae Farr killed him. I have a witness who can prove it. You play ball with me, and I play ball with you."

"I don't like that sort of a ball game," Mason said. "You call all the strikes and let me pitch all the balls."

"No, it isn't like that, Mason, honest. Look here, I'll put my cards on the table. Mae Farr bumped him. I think she was entitled to do it. I think a jury would think so, but it would be a lot better for her if she didn't have to go in front of a jury and tell all that stuff.

"You know, Penn was always on the make for her. I don't think she was any virgin, but she just didn't care for Penn. Perhaps she got a kick out of holding him at arm's length and watching him pant. Some women are like that."

"Go ahead," Mason said.

"Hell, do I have to draw you a diagram?"

"Yes."

Marley sighed and said, "Oh well, here it is. A certain party who shall be nameless was at the Yacht Club late last night and early this morning, sitting in an automobile waiting."

"For what?" Mason asked.

"What do you think?"

"I don't know."

"Well, we'll let it go at that then. She was waiting. She knew Penn. She knew me. She knew our boats. She didn't know Mae. While she was sitting in her car waiting and getting sore because she thought her boyfriend had stood her up, she saw the lights of a boat coming into the float. She thought at first it was the one she was waiting for, then she saw it was my cruiser, the *Atina*."

Mason shifted his eyes to watch the smoke which drifted upward from the tip of Marley's cigarette.

"The party handling the *Atina* didn't make such a good landing, scraped and bumped around a little bit, finally got the motors shut off, and jumped out with the mooring lines. She saw it was a girl. She didn't know the girl, but she got a good look at her face. Later on, she heard about the murder. She put two and two together. She told me about it. She described the girl. The description checks with Mae."

"Well," Mason said, "she—"

"Just a moment," Marley pleaded, holding up his hand. "I want you to have it absolutely straight. I had photographs taken on cruises, showing Mae Farr. I showed this girl the photographs. She's positive that Mae was the one who had my cruiser out."

"Well?" Mason asked.

"You can figure what that testimony will do to you," Marley said.

"It won't do a damn thing to me," Mason told him.

"Well, it will to your client."

"Testimony," Mason said, "is one thing. Conversation is another. Don't forget I have a right to cross-examine witnesses. There are a lot of questions I can think of right now that I'd like to ask this witness of yours. There'll probably be a lot more by the time I know more about the case."

"Sure there will," Marley said, his enunciation becoming more rapid. "That's what I'm getting at. You're dangerous, Mason. I know it. I'm not kidding myself a damn bit. You can probably beat the rap on Mae Farr. She's a good-looking baby, and jurors fall for that stuff.

She can put on a great story about fighting for her honor. It's a cinch. Good-looking women have lived with men for months and then killed them to defend their honor, and weeping juries have brought in verdicts exonerating the dames and asking for their telephone numbers afterwards. It's a cinch you can beat it."

"If I can beat the rap," Mason asked, "what have you got to trade?"

"Simply this," Marley told him. "If you play ball with me, there won't be any rap. They'll concentrate on Anders and try to pin the kill on him. They can't do it. They can get so far, and then it sticks. Anders didn't do it. Mae did."

"What makes you so positive?"

"After I heard what had happened to my boat, I went down and looked her over."

"When was that?"

"About two or three hours ago."

"What did you find?"

Marley said, "You know, Mason, I wasn't born yesterday."

"What did you find?" Mason repeated.

Marley said, "I found that a lock had been smashed, that someone had had the boat out. I always leave the boat with a full tank of gas. As nearly as I can tell from the gas gauge, she'd gone maybe ten miles. I know a little something about fingerprints—I learned it in the hard school of experience. I sprinkled some powder around where it would do the most good on the steering wheel, on the handle of the throttle, on the lighting switches."

"What did you find?" Mason asked.

"Fingerprints."

"Whose fingerprints?"

Marley shrugged and said, "I wouldn't know. It would be up to the police to tell whose fingerprints they were."

"What's your proposition?" Mason asked.

Marley said, "I'll give you five grand in cash right now. I'll take an oiled cloth, go down and scrub off every fingerprint on the boat. I'll buy this witness a ticket to Australia, and let her stay there until the case is over. You advise me about how to wind up the partnership business."

"Why can't any attorney do that?"

"I tell you, it's a mess. I've been careless. I've relied too much on conversation and not enough on records. I did virtually all of the business recently. Penn got so he left things more and more to me."

"Why do you think I could handle the widow better than any other lawyer?" Mason asked.

"You have the reputation. What's more, you have the knowledge, and if she gets too tough, you could bring a little pressure to bear on her. You know, let her feel that you were going to rip her wide open when she came into court to testify. Penn had some stuff on Juanita. She's nobody's fool. She knows that."

Mason said, "That's all of your proposition?"

Marley nodded.

"Pardon me a minute," Mason said as he rang the buzzer for Della Street.

When she opened the door, he said, with a nod to Frank Marley, "Mr. Marley will be leaving shortly. Tell Drake that he can come back. And tell him to make adequate preparations to report progress on everything that happens from now on. Emphasize *everything*. Do you understand?"

She nodded. "I'll tell him, Mr. Mason. Is there anything else?"

Mason shook his head and she closed the door.

"Sorry for the interruption," Mason said, turning back to face Marley. "I don't like your proposition."

"I could up the cash a little—not very much because I'm short right now, and Penn's death is going to . . ."

90

"No," Mason said, "it isn't the cash."

"What is it?"

"It's the idea."

"What idea?"

"Of suppressing evidence, for one thing."

Marley looked at him in surprise. "You mean to say that you're going chicken on a little thing that's done every day of the week?"

"You can call it that if you want to."

Marley said, "Well, look. We don't have to do anything. We can simply . . ."

Mason shook his head.

"Listen," Marley said, "this is on the square. There's just the two of us here. It isn't any trap. It's a straightout business proposition."

Again Mason shook his head.

"For God's sake," Marley said, "don't tell me you're going to pull that line. If you're going to act like that, it's your duty to see that this witness tells her story to the police."

"It may be at that."

Marley said, "Look here, Mason, don't be a fool. You're in business. You know which side of the bread has the butter."

Mason said, "From where I sit, it doesn't seem to be your side."

Marley said indignantly, "You mean I'm apt to sell you out? You mean you think you can't trust me?"

Mason said, "I'm not interested."

"Think it over for an hour or two," Marley said. "I think you'll figure it's the only thing to do. Anders has spilled his guts. You're in a spot. I'm in a spot. Mae Farr is in a spot. If we play this thing right, we can all get off the spot."

Mason said coldly, "I like to lead my own aces, Marley."

Marley said, "I know. You think I'm bluffing. You

think there isn't any witness. You think that I'd simply go down and clean the inside of the yacht, tell you I'd sent the witness to Australia, and be sitting pretty."

"You could do just that," Mason pointed out.

"Don't be a damn fool," Marley said.

"I'll try not to," Mason assured him.

Marley sighed, said, "Cripes, if you haven't any better sense than that, I don't want you for an attorney. I think you're vastly overrated."

"Sometimes I think so myself," Mason said.

Marley started for the door, paused with his hand on the knob to look back at Mason. "No," he said thoughtfully, "you aren't dumb. You're smart. You figure you can make *me* the fall guy. Well, think again, Mason."

Frank Marley jerked open the door, then slammed it shut behind him.

Mason picked up the desk telephone and said to the operator in the outer office, "Get Della Street for me right away."

Almost immediately he heard Della's voice on the line. "Okay, Chief, what is it?"

"Did you get my message straight for Paul Drake?"

"I think so. You meant that you wanted Marley shadowed?"

"Yes. I was wondering if you'd get it."

"Two operatives will be in the lobby," she said. "Another operative is being planted at the elevator. She'll put the finger on Marley for the two detectives downstairs. Drake had to work fast, but he did it."

"Good girl," Mason said.

9

■

It lacked ten minutes until five o'clock when Paul
Drake entered Mason's office with news. "Marley," he
said, "left here and went directly to the Balkan Apartments on Windstrom Avenue. He kept buzzing the
apartment of Hazel Tooms until he decided he was
drawing a blank. Then he started out toward the harbor on Figueroa Street. My operatives are tailing him.
Does this Tooms girl mean anything to you?"

"Not so far," Mason said. "Look her up. See who she
is. See if she's a nurse."

"Okay. Here's something else. The police have found
the murder gun."

"They're certain?"

"Yes. The bullets tally exactly."

"Where did they find it?"

"That's the funny thing," Drake said. "They found it
right where Anders says he threw the gun."

"What do you mean?"

"Get this," Drake said. "The highway is banked way up
at that particular place, probably eight or ten feet above
the level of the surrounding country. There's a deep drainage ditch on each side of the highway."

"I know," Mason said. "Just how did they find the gun
and just where did they find it?"

"Anders stood on that highway and threw it as hard
as he could throw it," Drake said. "The gun evidently
hit the high tension post on the side of the road and
dropped back into the ditch. It started to rain a short
time later, and quite a bit of water gathered in the
drainage ditch. During wet weather, water stands in
there two or three feet deep. The water went down this

afternoon, and some smart photographer who had been sent out to photograph your footprints happened to notice it lying there in the water.

"It's a thirty-eight-caliber Colt, police-positive. Police rushed a test bullet through it, and compared it with the fatal bullet. They were both fired by the same gun."

Mason said, "What does Anders have to say to that?"

"I don't know," Drake said. "It doesn't make very much difference what he does have to say to it. It puts him in an awful spot."

"Numbers on the gun?" Mason asked.

"I guess so. Remember, Perry, this is last-minute news, hot off the wire. My friend on the newspaper handed it to me as a flash."

"Well," Mason said, "I guess they'll turn Mae Farr loose now. I filed *habeas corpus* on her."

"They'll want to hold her as a witness," Drake said.

"They will and they won't. She cuts both ways. Once they can pin the kill on Anders, it's up to him to show the circumstances which would justify or extenuate his actions. That means it's up to him to keep Mae Farr where he can put his finger on her. She's more important to the defense than to the prosecution.

"Listen, Paul, get busy on that Tooms girl, find out all you can about her. Keep men on Marley and see if you can scare up anything more on Eversel. How about Mrs. Wentworth? I presume the police have been checking on her?"

"I guess so. She went up to the D.A.'s office shortly after noon, was in there for about an hour. As I get it, she took it right on the chin, said that it was a shame that it had to happen, that naturally she regretted it, that she and Wentworth were estranged, that she wasn't going to pretend they were good friends any longer, that differences over property affairs had become very bitter, that naturally his death came as a shock to her.

"My newspaper friend slipped me a bunch of photographs. Among them is a swell one of Juanita Wentworth just leaving her automobile in front of the courthouse."

"Why leaving the automobile?" Mason asked.

Drake said, "These newspaper photographers are instructed to get lots of leg in the pictures. You can't very well pose a widow that way. It's in poor taste. So they got a 'candid camera' shot just as she was getting out of the automobile."

"I see," Mason said, and then added, after a moment, "How about her story, Paul? Did the D.A.'s office ask her for more particulars, or did they just hit the high spots?"

"I don't know just what"—Della Street slipped through the door from the outer office. Drake broke off to glance up at her for a moment, then finished quickly—"what they talked about, Perry."

Della said, "Mae Farr's in the office."

Mason jerked his head toward the door. "Beat it, Paul," he said. "I want to get the lowdown on some stuff. Anything she tells me is privileged unless a third party like yourself overhears it. Then it is no longer privileged communication and we might all be in a spot later on. Keep working on things and dig up all the information you can."

"I will," Drake said, "and you'd better work fast with Mae Farr, Perry."

"Meaning what?"

"Meaning that she's outside now, but I have a hunch she won't stay out long."

"Why, Paul?"

"Just the way things are looking," Drake said. "I'm on my way, Perry."

"So long," Mason said, and nodded to Della Street.

Della went out and brought Mae Farr into the office. She crossed over to Perry Mason, her head held high, a defiant smile on her lips. "Hello," she said. "Are we speaking or aren't we?"

"Why not?" Mason asked. Sit down and have a cigarette."

"Do you want me?" Della asked.

Mason shook his head. "And see that we're not disturbed, Della."

"I'm closing up the office now," she said, and walked swiftly through the door to the outer offices.

"Why," Mason asked Mae Farr, "shouldn't we be speaking?"

"I'm afraid I got you in something of a spot."

"That's nothing. I'm accustomed to spots. What did you tell the police?"

"Not a thing."

"What do you mean by that?"

"Exactly what I said. I told them nothing."

"Did they read Anders' statement to you?"

"They told me about what he'd said first—with a lot of variations of their own, and then they let me see their signed statement, which differed quite a bit from what they'd said it was."

"And you told them absolutely nothing?"

"Not a thing. I said that I was a working girl with my reputation to think of, and I didn't care to make any statement whatever."

"What did they say to that?"

"They said that I'd get in more deeply than ever by adopting that sort of an attitude. I told them that was fine. They've given me a subpoena to appear before a grand jury. They say I'll have to talk then. Will I?"

"Probably," Mason said. "If you didn't kill him, you'd better talk."

"I didn't kill him."

"Did Anders kill him?"

"I can't believe he did, but if he didn't, who did?"

Mason said, "Let's go back to last night. You started back to town with me. Then you went on ahead. Now then, what did you do after that?"

"Kept right on going to town," she said.

"To your apartment?"

"Yes."

"Then what?"

"Then this morning detectives from the Homicide Squad came and got me out of bed, and held me for questioning."

Mason said, "You didn't, by any chance, turn around after you left me and double back to the Yacht Club, did you?"

"Good heavens, no! Why?"

"Someone tried to tell me you did."

"Who?"

"A man by the name of Marley. Do you know him?"

"Oh, Frank," she said scornfully, and then, after a moment, "What does he know about me?"

"Don't you know him?"

"Yes. I mean, what does he know about me being down at the Yacht Club?"

"He says you were. He says you were the one who took his cruiser out."

"Nonsense," she said. He was out himself, and he's trying to cover up."

"What makes you say he was out in the boat?"

"Because he has one of those devious minds that never approaches anything directly. He works around in a circle. If you want to know where he's going, you never look in the direction in which he's headed."

"I see," Mason said with a smile.

"He's clever," she added hastily. "Don't overlook that."

"You know him fairly well?"

"Yes."

"Seen a good deal of him?"

"Too much," she said.

"You don't like him?"

"I hate the ground he walks on."

Mason said, "Let's get things straight, Mae. How well did you know Penn Wentworth?"

"Too damn well."

"His wife?"

"I've never met her."

"Was Frank Marley playing around with Wentworth's wife?"

"I wouldn't know," she said.

"Would you have any ideas on the subject?"

"If Juanita Wentworth left the door open, Frank Marley would walk in," she said.

"Why," Mason asked, "do you hate him? Did he ever make a pass at you?"

"Lord, yes—and never got even halfway to first base."

"Is that why you dislike him?"

"No." She met his eyes steadily and said, "I may as well be frank with you. I don't object to men making passes at me. I like it if they go about it in the right way. I don't like it if they whine about it or try to appeal to my sympathies. I don't like Frank Marley because of his dishonesty—no, not his dishonesty either. I don't object to a man cutting corners if he is clever about it. I've known men who weren't exactly honest. Some of them have fascinated me. What I don't like about Frank is his sneaky, underhanded intrigue. You just can't tell about him. He'll be suave and friendly and reach around you as though to put a friendly arm around your waist, and there'll be a knife in his hand. He'll stick it in to the hilt, and never change expression. He never raises his voice, never bats an eyelash, never gets flustered. And he's dangerous."

Mason said, "Let's talk about you for a while."

"What about me?"

"Quite a lot of things," Mason said, "for instance, about what happened on the *Pennwent*."

"Well, what about it?"

Mason said, "When you told me about that, your boyfriend was with you."

"Well?" she asked.

"Did you," Mason asked, "sort of expurgate the account because he was there?"

She stared steadily at him and said, "No. It would take more than Hal Anders to make me lie. Look here, Mr. Mason, I'm going to tell you something about myself. I pay my own way as I go through the world, and I want the privilege of living my own life. I left North Mesa because I couldn't do just that. I have my own code, my own creed, and my own ideas. I try to be true to them, all of them. I hate hypocrisy. I like fair play. I want to live my own life in my own way, and I'm willing to let other people live their lives in their way."

"How about Anders?"

"Anders wanted me to marry him. I thought for a while I was going to. I changed my mind. I hate weak men."

"What's wrong with Anders?"

"What isn't wrong with him," she said bitterly, and then added, after a moment, "Oh, he's all right, but he needs a lot of fixing. He can't get along without having someone pat him on the back and tell him he's doing all right, that he's a wonderful young man, and all that stuff.

"Look at what happened in this case. You told him what to do. You told him particularly to go to his hotel and stay there until he heard from you. Did he do it? He did not. He never even got as far as the hotel. He had to have someone else give him advice. That's the trouble with him. He's never learned to stand on his own two feet and take things as they come."

Mason said, "I'm not certain but what you judge him too harshly."

"Maybe I do," she admitted.

"Don't you think perhaps he's tried to advise you, tried

99

to interfere with your life, and you resented that, but that you really care a lot for him and are trying all the harder to fan your resentment into flame because the fuel doesn't want to burn?"

She smiled and said, "You may be right at that. I've always resented him because he was so darn *good*. Everyone pointed him out as a model young man. He didn't drink, didn't smoke, didn't gamble, worked hard, was nice to old ladies, kept his lodge dues paid, his hair cut and his nails clean. He read all the best books, listened to the best music, raised the best stock, and got the best prices.

"Everything he ever does is carefully worked out and programmed—and it's always on the advice of someone else. The horticultural commissioner tells him about how to handle his land. His lawyer tells him about his contracts. His banker tells him about how to handle his finances. That's what makes me so darn *tired* of him. He's always attentive, always learning, always right, but he's always right because he's taken the advice of someone who knew. He has good judgment. He usually knows which is the best advice and he acts on it."

"Don't we all live our lives that way?" Mason asked. "At any rate, to a greater or lesser extent?"

"I don't," she said simply, and then added, with feeling, "and I don't want to."

"You resented his coming to the city to look you up?"

"Yes, I did. It was very decent of him to offer to pay the amount of that check, but I'm perfectly capable of living my own life. If I get into something, I want to get out of it through my own efforts. If I can't, I want to stay there. I don't want to have Hal Anders rushing into the city to lift me up out of the gutter, brush the mud off my clothes, smile sweetly down at me, and say, 'Won't you come home now, Mae, marry me, settle down, and live happily ever after?' "

"He still wants you to marry him?"

"Of course. He's rather single-minded when he gets an idea in his head."

"You don't intend to?"

"I do not. I suppose I'm an ingrate. I know I'm in a jam. I suppose he'll come to my rescue with money and moral support, and I should be grateful and fall in his arms when it's all over. Well, just for your personal, private information, Mr. Perry Mason, I'm not going to do anything of the sort."

"All right," Mason said. "Let's talk about what happened on the yacht."

"I've told you what happened."

"You said Wentworth was wearing his underclothes."

"He was."

"When the body was found, it was fully clothed."

"I can't help that," she said. "When he was shot, he was wearing his underwear, and that's all."

"How did it start?"

"Oh, he said he had to take a cruise that night and asked me if I'd excuse him while he changed his clothes and put on his overalls. He said he had some work to do on the motors. He went to the after cabin to change. He'd left the door open. I didn't know it. I strolled back towards the engine room. I could look right in the cabin where he was changing. I guess that gave him ideas. He started working on me instead of the engines."

"How loudly did you scream?"

"I didn't know I screamed," she said. "Hal says I did. I think he's cockeyed. I think I did a little cussing, some kicking, and a little scratching and biting. If I screamed, I was screaming at Penn and not for help. I got myself aboard that yacht, and I could get myself off of it. I never was one to yell much for help."

"Were you nervous, hysterical?"

"Me?" she asked in surprise.

"Yes."

"Good Lord, no! I was being crowded into a corner," she said, "and I was getting pretty tired. I didn't know how much longer I was going to hold out. Look, Mr. Mason, I've fought men off before, and I'll probably do it again."

"Do you," Mason asked, "inspire men to violence?"

"I don't think so," she said. "A lot of men try caveman tactics because a lot of girls fall for them. I don't. The minute a man starts pushing me around, I want to hit him with anything I can get my hands on. I think I have more trouble that way than most girls because I'm inclined to be independent, and men resent that. A lot of girls make a habit of saying 'no' in such a way they make the man like it. When I say 'no,' I say 'NO.' I don't give a hang whether he likes it or doesn't like it."

"When did you see Frank Marley last?"

"Sunday, a week ago."

"Where?"

"We went on a cruise—a bunch of us."

"Was Wentworth along?"

"Yes."

"On the *Pennwent?*"

"No," she said, "on Marley's cruiser, the *Atina*. We took a quick run over to Catalina."

"Can you run that boat?"

"Yes. I brought it back all the way. I wish I could like Marley as well as I do his boat. It's a honey."

"What about you and Wentworth?"

She said, "We met some time ago. I did some work for him. I saw he was taking quite an interest in me. He asked me to go on a cruise. You know what those cruises are apt to be. I told him straight from the shoulder. He said it was okay by him. All he wanted was my company. I went. Okay, he was going to open up a bookmaking office. It was against the law, but he claimed he had it squared with the officers. He wanted

102

me to be in the place to class it up and sort of check on Marley. He knew that Marley's line didn't go across with me, and he was a little suspicious of Frank. Frank was handling most of the money end of the business. Penn thought it would be a good idea to have someone around who could check up on him.

"To tell you the truth, I don't think Frank liked the idea. If you started prodding around in Frank's accounts, I think you'd find something rotten. I told Penn that."

"What did Penn say?" Mason asked.

"Not very much. He told me I was wrong, but I could see he was turning what I'd said over in his mind."

"And the clothes?" Mason asked.

She said, "I get mad every time I think about that. It was a straight business proposition from first to last. Wentworth wasn't to pay for those clothes unless something happened and I didn't go to work. I was to go to work and pay the bill out of my salary in installments. The whole thing was explained to the credit manager at the time the account was opened. I tell you it was a business proposition."

"But you didn't pay for the clothes?"

"No, of course not. I never went to work. There was a shake-up in city politics. The men they thought they could control were transferred around to other districts. They didn't give up the idea entirely but marked time trying to establish new contacts.

"Well, that was the understanding we had when he put the proposition up to me. I was out of work. I wasn't to draw any regular salary until the place opened. I was to spend a good deal of time with Penn, meeting his friends and getting to know who they were. Penn was to send my sister a small check every three weeks and to pay my living expenses. I was to have enough clothes to make a good impression. In a way, I was to be the official hostess on his yachting parties.

"I didn't need anyone to tell me what it looked like. It looked like the devil. I didn't need anyone to tell me that in the back of Penn's mind was the idea that I'd become dependent on him, get under his control, and become his mistress. I didn't care what was in his mind. I knew what was in my mind. I didn't sail under any false colors. I told him so right at the start. He knew the way I felt. He thought he could make me change. All right, it was a fair deal and no favors."

"But your family?" Mason asked.

"There the shoe pinched. I was out of work and couldn't get any satisfactory job. I figured this would open up into something that would pay. I also knew darn well that there was a chance the place might be raided and I'd find myself dragged into court. I didn't think they'd do anything to me, but I didn't know. I knew it would hurt Mother terribly if she thought I was mixed up in a business like that. I didn't want to lie to them, so I just quit writing. But I also knew Sylvia needed some help with finances, so I arranged to have Penn send her some money until my regular salary began. By that time, I expected to have money to send her. Now then, that's the story."

Mason said, "It's a good story if it's true."

Her eyes darkened.

"Don't get excited," Mason said. "I'm talking particularly about what happened after you left me. A witness will claim that you took Frank Marley's cruiser out for a spin."

"That *I* did?"

"Yes."

"When?"

"Sometime after we made our trip to the Yacht Club."

"I did not."

"The witness says you did."

"The witness lies. What in the name of reason would I want with Frank Marley's boat?"

Mason said, "If Hal Anders had gone back to the *Pennwent*, instead of going to his hotel, and had taken it out to sea and started it heading down the coast in the direction of Ensenada, you *could* have taken Marley's cruiser and gone out to pick him up. The *Atina* was at least twice as fast as the *Pennwent*."

"That's absurd. Hal went directly to North Mesa so he could consult his old family lawyer."

"He went to North Mesa all right," Mason said. "I'm not so certain about the direct part of it."

"Well, I've told you the truth."

Mason got up, reached for his hat, and said, "Okay, we'll let it go at that."

"What do you want me to do?" she asked.

Mason said, "Go back to your apartment, act just as though nothing had happened. Newspaper reporters will call on you. People will ask questions. Photographers will want pictures. Give them all the pictures they want. Remember newspapermen are working for a living. They're sent out to get stories, pictures, and interviews. If they come back with something good, the boss pats them on the back. If they come back without anything, the boss snarls at them. So give them something to come back with. Let them pose you any way they want to, give them all the pictures they want, and tell them that you're not discussing the case."

"I get you," she said.

"As far as the newspaper reporters are concerned," Mason said, "tell them all about your romance with Hal Anders."

"It wasn't any romance."

"That's what I want you to tell them. Tell them just about the way you've told it to me."

"About his being weak and always asking for advice—"

"No, not that," Mason interrupted. "The part about how he's such a model young man who never makes any mistakes and how you got tired of it all. You wanted to come to the city and see life for yourself. And tell them all about Wentworth's proposition that you should go to work for him, only don't let on that you knew it was a bookmaking business. Simply say that it was a downtown office he intended to open up, and he wouldn't tell you very much about what it was only that it was to handle some of his investments. But about the things that happened last night, keep mum. You'd like to talk, but your attorney has told you to say absolutely nothing."

"In other words," she said, "I'm to give them something they can turn into copy, is that it?"

"That's right."

"Okay, I'll do that little thing."

"How about it?" Mason asked. "Are you nervous and upset?"

She shook her head and smiled. "It's all part of the game," she said. "Sometimes you're on top and things are easy. Sometimes you're on the bottom. There's no need to let it worry you."

Abruptly, she thrust out her hand, smiled up into his face, and said, "Good night, Mr. Mason."

Mason stood for a moment holding her hand, looking down into her eyes. "Did they," he asked, "try to browbeat you, try to make you nervous?"

"Did they?" She laughed. "All of them yelled questions at me and asked me to reenact what happened at the time of the shooting, and then when that failed, accused me of having been his mistress and lying to Hal about it because I wanted to marry Hal in order to be on financial easy street. I guess they tried everything, Mr. Mason."

Mason grinned and said, "I guess they did. Okay, on your way. Think you can remember all I've told you?"

"Sure," she said.

She flashed him a quick smile from the door, then Mason could hear her heels click . . . clack . . . click . . . clacking down the corridor toward the elevator.

Mason put on his hat, went out to the other office, and said, "All right, Della, I'm going out into the highways and byways. Get yourself some dinner and stick around the telephone."

She reached up to take possession of his right hand, caressing it with hers. "You'll be careful, Chief?" she asked.

Smiling down at her, he once more shook his head.

She laughed and said, "I could have saved my breath, but keep your eyes peeled, and if there's anything I can do, let me know."

"Okay, Della, but I want you to keep out of circulation for a little while. I don't want to have them drag you into the case. They've subpoenaed Mae Farr to appear before the grand jury. They'll probably subpoena me."

"And me?" she asked.

Mason nodded.

"What'll we tell them?"

Mason said, "We won't commit any perjury. We won't play into their hands. And we won't betray the interests of our clients. We'll generally adopt the position that just about everything that happened was a privileged communication, confidential, and not the subject of a grand jury investigation. That'll raise a lot of technical points. Oh, we'll come out all right, Della."

"I suppose you want me to say nothing."

"Be like the clam," Mason said.

"At high tide?"

"What's the difference?" he asked.

"You gather clams at *low* tide."

"Right," Mason said. "Be like a clam at high tide."

As the door closed behind him, the telephone rang. Della picked up the receiver and answered.

"Hello, beautiful," said Paul Drake. "Let me speak to the boss."

"He's just stepped out," said Della, "and I think he is looking for action."

"Oh, oh," said Paul. "I was waiting for him to give me a ring after Mae Farr left. The D.A. has sent the story out. The papers aren't mentioning names right now because they're afraid, but the D.A.'s office is mentioning names. They state that they're prepared to prove Mason was out last night looking for that gun, that he's going to be subpoenaed to appear before the grand jury, and that in the meantime he's being kept under the closest surveillance. He—"

Della said, "Gosh! Let me try to catch him at the elevator, Paul."

She slammed down the receiver, dashed out of the door, raced down the corridor to the elevators, and frantically jabbed at the button. When one of the elevators stopped, she said breathlessly to the operator, "Listen, Sam, rush me down to the ground floor, will you, please? I have to get there right away."

The elevator operator grinned, nodded, and, disregarding the curious stares of the other passengers as well as various stop signals along the way, dropped the cage swiftly to the lower corridor.

Della pushed people to one side, running toward the street exit. She was just in time to see Mason enter a taxicab fifty feet down the street. She called to him, but he couldn't hear her. The taxicab swung out into traffic. Two men in plainclothes, sitting in an automobile parked in front of a fireplug, eased their car into motion and in behind the taxicab.

Della looked quickly up and down the street, could find no cab in sight. A red traffic signal held up traffic coming her way while the cab containing Mason and the car with the two officers turned to the right at the next intersection and were swallowed up in traffic.

Della Street turned and went slowly back to the office.

10

■

MASON DISCHARGED the taxicab a block from the Balkan Apartments and reconnoitered carefully. The two plainclothesmen who had followed the taxicab drove on past without so much as a look in Mason's direction. Mason walked the block to the apartment house and looked at the directory for the name of Hazel Tooms.

As he pressed the button opposite her name, a man came walking briskly down the street from the opposite direction, turned into the apartment house, and fished in his pocket for a latchkey.

The electric door release buzzed, and the man who had been looking for his latchkey pushed against the door and went on in. Mason followed him, passed him in the corridor, walked to the elevator, and went to the fifth floor. He found 521 near the end of the corridor and tapped gently on the panels of the door.

The young woman who opened the door was taller than average and was dressed in lounging pajamas. She carried herself firmly erect. Her brownish hair had highlights. Her eyes, blue and cautious, surveyed Perry Mason in frank appraisal. There was neither nervousness nor fear in her manner. She seemed quite capable of taking care of herself in any emergency.

"I don't know you," she said.

"A situation which I wish to remedy at once," Mason replied, lifting his hat and bowing.

She looked him over from head to foot, then stood to one side. "Come in," she said.

When Mason had entered the apartment, she closed the door, indicated a chair, and then, instead of seating herself, stood with her back to the door, her hands on the knob.

"All right," she said. "What is it?"

Mason said, "My name is Mason. Does that mean anything to you?"

"Not a thing. If this is a mash, save your breath. I don't go out with strangers."

Mason said, "I'm doing a little investigating."

"Oh," she said.

"'I have reason to believe," Mason went on, "that you have some information in which I'd be interested."

"What about?"

"About the *Pennwent*."

"What about it?"

"When you saw it last and about Frank Marley's *Atina* and when you saw it last."

"A detective?" she asked.

"Not exactly," Mason said.

"What's your angle?"

"I'm representing someone who wants the facts."

"What's in it for me?"

"Nothing."

She left the door then and sat down across from Perry Mason. She crossed her legs and hugged one knee with the interlaced fingers of large, capable hands. "Pardon me for being cautious," she said, "but you read so much stuff these days of men getting into women's apartments, slugging them over the head, choking them, and playful little practices of that sort, and I was taking no chances."

"Did I," Mason asked, "look like one of those?"

"I don't know," she said. "I don't know what they look like."

Mason laughed. Hazel Tooms smiled slightly.

"Well," Mason said, "let's get back to my question."

"About the boats?"

"Yes."

"What about them?"

"When did you see Frank Marley's cruiser last?"

She smiled and said, "Really, Mr. Mason, I'd prefer to get back to *my* original question."

"What's that?"

"What's in it for me?"

"Exactly what I told you the first time," Mason said. "Nothing."

"Then why should I answer?" she asked.

"Let's look at it another way," Mason suggested, with a slight twinkle in his eye. "Why *shouldn't* you answer?"

She said, "Charity may begin at home, but it ends up in the poorhouse."

Mason said, "All right. I'll put my cards on the table."

"Aces first, please," she said.

"I'm a lawyer. I'm representing a Miss Mae Farr in connection with—"

"Oh, you're *Perry* Mason."

He nodded.

"Why didn't you say so in the first place?"

"I didn't think it would do any good."

She looked at him, her brows puckered together, her head tilted slightly to one side. "Well," she said at length, "so *you're* Perry Mason."

Mason said nothing.

"And interested in information you think I have. Is that information going to get me in trouble?"

"I don't know," Mason said.

"Listen," she told him, "I don't want to go on the witness stand."

"You're not on the witness stand now."

"No, but you might put me there."

"Again, I might not."

"Would you promise not to?"

"No."

She caressed her knee with the tips of her fingers, her eyes distant and preoccupied with a survey of the possibilities of the situation. Abruptly, she brought her eyes into hard, sharp focus on the lawyer's face, then said, "All right, I'm going to take a chance. I'm strong on taking chances."

Mason settled back in the chair and shifted his eyes slightly so that she could talk without being conscious of his gaze.

She said, "I can't go on the witness stand because a smart lawyer would make me out a sorry figure. I've always loved the outdoors—tennis, riding, skiing, all sports. Especially, I like yachting. You don't get invited on boat trips by cultivating the company of impecunious young men of regular habits and virtuous intentions.

"You've heard of gold diggers? Well, I guess I'm a yacht digger. Whenever there was a cruise over to Catalina, I met all the yachtsmen I could. Whenever they wanted my telephone number, I gave it to them. That's all I give them, my telephone number, my company, and a lot of laughs.

"Lots of times yachtsmen want girls along who are good sports, know something about handling a boat, are willing to do a good share of the work, and can keep the gang laughing.

"I suppose I could have used the same amount of mental effort in some commercial activity and made money. I work like the devil thinking up wisecracks, games, stunts, and how to drink a lot without getting too awfully drunk. If you've never tried it, eating a lot of butter before the drinking starts is a swell stunt."

"I have a recipe which beats that," Mason said.

"You have?"

"Yes."

"Be a good sport and give it to me. That butter stunt is the best I've ever found."

Mason said, "Mine is more simple. I don't drink much after the drinking starts."

"Oh," she said, her voice showing disappointment. "I thought you were really going to say something."

Mason said, "Don't let me interrupt you."

"I won't—not again. Well, Mr. Mason, here's the low-down. Penn Wentworth took a shine to me. He was on the make. When you say 'no' to Penn, he starts wrestling, and when he wrestles, he gets out of control. Personally, I don't like to be manhandled. My eyes, my judgment of distance, and my timing are all pretty good. I just won a tennis championship the other day.

"Well, when the party got just so rough, I warned him. Warning didn't do any good. He was past that point. So I slipped my shoe off, doubled up my leg, waited my chance, and shot my heel straight to the chin."

"Connect?" Mason asked.

"Of course I connected."

"What happened to Wentworth?"

She said, "I thought I'd killed him. I poured water on his face, rubbed his chest and ribs, and fed him brandy with a teaspoon. It seemed like an hour before he came around, and he was still punch-drunk for another thirty minutes."

"Then what?" Mason asked. "Did he come up for round two, or did he toss in the towel when the bell rang?"

She grinned and said, "He tossed in the towel, and it made the start of a swell friendship. I got so I cared a lot for him after that, and he respected me. We had one of those friendships that are so rare between a man and a woman, just perfect pals. He found out that I liked boats, and he liked to have me with him. Occasionally, he'd go off on a trip just by himself when he didn't want anyone around to bother him and talk to him. He never cared about yachting as yachting but used the yacht simply for incidental pleasure—attending the cruises, staging parties, and things of that sort. That's why he had all those gadgets on the *Pennwent*.

"This is the part you're not going to believe. However, it happens to be the truth. When Wentworth would have a fit of the blues, he liked to go on a cruise. He'd leave the handling of the boat pretty much up to me. He'd let me do the cooking. Sometimes we'd take an entire cruise without saying a word except a few comments about what he wanted to eat and about handling the boat. That suited me right down to the ground. I love to head out into the ocean with my hands on the wheel. It gives me a thrill, a sense of power. I know the ocean is cruel and merciless. I know that you can't make any mistakes with the ocean. I like to play that kind of a game."

She hesitated a moment, studying Mason's face, apparently waiting for some comment. He made none. She said, "Naturally, I got to know Frank Marley. He's different from Penn. Frank never made a pass at me. If he ever does, he'll have all the dice loaded against me. He waits and watches and thinks and schemes, and you never know what he's thinking about from what he says.

"Penn was a good egg. A girl couldn't trust herself around Penn Wentworth for five minutes. He'd try a line, and if that didn't work, he'd try massage, and if that didn't work, he'd get rough. But there was one thing about Penn. You always knew where he stood, and he was never a hypocrite. Any girl who went out with Penn Wentworth knew that Penn was—well, sticky. Once you got past that first round with him, he made a swell friend. Penn had a lot to him. He was shrewd and fair. He had a sense of humor, and he could be a very good companion when he didn't have the blues.

114

When he had the blues, he wanted you to leave him alone, and he'd leave you alone.

"Frank Marley was the exact opposite. I've been out with Frank a lot of times. I've handled his boat a lot. He'd be sitting or standing somewhere nearby all the time, smoking cigarettes and watching me with half-closed eyes through the cigarette smoke. He was always a perfect gentleman, always quiet, always well behaved—and always waiting."

She stopped to study Mason's face curiously, then said, "Oh, go ahead and look at me. I'll keep on talking just the same."

"No," Mason said. "I'm listening. I listen with my ears and look with my eyes. I can't do two things at once and really concentrate on them. Right now, I'm listening to your voice."

"Don't you think you can tell more about a woman by watching her when she talks than by listening to what she says?"

"Not always," Mason said. "A lawyer trains himself to listen. Witnesses have usually rehearsed their story pretty well—at least to the extent of making the mannerisms and gestures more or less mechanical, but they rehearse silently. People really should cultivate the art of talking to themselves. They'd learn a lot about voices if they did."

She laughed and said, "You make me feel frightfully naked—sitting there with your head turned and your ears taking in every word."

"I didn't intend to. You have a very observing mind."

"Think so?"

"Yes."

"Thanks."

"Well," Mason said, "that's that. We were talking about Frank Marley's boat."

"I was talking about the yachts and the men," she said. "Late in the afternoon, Wentworth called and said he'd

115

like to see me. I drove down and went aboard. He said that he had to be in San Diego the next day for an appointment with his wife. He told me that he had finally decided to give her an ultimatum: either she would give him a divorce on reasonable terms or he would sue Sid Eversel for alienation of affections. Then he suggested that I go with him and that we take the *Pennwent* to Ensenada. He'd drive to San Diego to meet his wife. Of course, I'd stay aboard; he didn't want his wife to know I was with him.

"Well," she said, "that suited me right down to the ground. I told Penn I'd have to go get some clothes and provisions we needed. He gave me some money and told me to stop on the way back and pick up the supplies at one of the all-night markets. As soon as I returned, we'd sail.

"I drove back. The *Pennwent* was gone. I thought perhaps he'd taken it out for a trial spin. He'd never stood me up. Ours wasn't that sort of a friendship. I knew he wanted me to sail the boat for him. I stuck around. I thought for a while I'd go over and see if anyone was aboard Frank Marley's boat, then I saw that it, too, was gone.

"Ordinarily, I wouldn't have waited very long, but I did want that trip to Ensenada, and I felt certain that anything that had taken Penn away would be a real emergency. I knew that he'd have left word if he'd had to pull out without me.

"There's a message board up by the clubhouse, a place with a lot of little mailboxes where people can leave messages for the various yachts. I looked in Penn's box. There wasn't any message. I went back to the car and waited some more."

"Just a minute," Mason interrupted. "What time was all this?"

"I don't know what time it was," she said. "I remember it started to rain when I was buying the groceries. Does that mean anything?"

Mason nodded.

She said, "I don't think it rained down at the Club for half or three-quarters of an hour after that. The showers were drifting in from the mountains.

"Well, I dropped off to sleep, sitting there in the car and dozing. I'd been playing tennis all afternoon—a small tournament—amateur stuff. I'd won the medal for second place in the women's division, and the girl who'd beat me had done every dirty trick in the cards. God, how I hated to lose to that woman.

"I guess I had the blues myself. Anyhow, the thought of that boat trip down to Ensenada soothed my mind. I kept waiting and dozing. Then I heard a boat coming in. I thought it was the *Pennwent*. I opened the door and started to get out of the car. Then I saw it was Frank Marley's *Atina*. I figured he'd know where Penn was, but I wasn't certain Marley was alone. You know yachting etiquette is a little different from other stuff. You wait to make certain the man's alone or else you give him a chance to make the play.

"Well, first rattle out of the box, this girl showed on deck, running ashore with the lines. I could tell from the way the boat was handled that she was alone on it. Boy oh boy, I sure looked her over."

"Jealous?" Mason asked.

She said, "It might add up to that. I figured if Frank Marley was generous enough in his softer moments to let a girl take his cruiser and just sail out on parties of her own—well, it was an interesting idea."

"Did you recognize this girl?"

"Not then," she said. "I've found out since that it was Mae Farr."

"How do you know?"

"I've seen photographs of her."

"Who showed them to you?"

117

"That," she said, "is something we won't discuss right now. I haven't that party's permission."

"Was it Frank Marley?" Mason asked.

"We won't discuss it."

"Then what?" Mason asked.

"I waited about half an hour after the girl had left," Hazel Tooms said, "and then gave it up as a bad job. I figured something had happened and Penn had been called away without even having time to leave a message for me. I came home, climbed into a hot tub, and then went to bed."

Mason said, "You jumped at this trip to Ensenada?"

"Yes."

"You were going alone with Wentworth?"

"That's what I said."

"That," Mason observed, "would be rather bad for the sake of appearances."

"Well, what of it?" she asked defiantly.

"Exactly what I was getting at," Mason said. "You don't seem to care much for appearances."

"I don't give a damn for them."

"You have your own car?"

"Such as it is, yes."

"And you're able to leave on a moment's notice to go on trips?"

"What are you getting at?" she asked.

Mason smiled and said, "Perhaps it's my habit of leading up to something through cross-examination. What I'm really trying to find out is what are your means of support?"

"Oh," she said, "that. I guess a lawyer could put me in a funny position before a jury with a line of questions like that, couldn't he?"

Mason nodded.

"Well," she said, and hesitated.

"Go ahead," Mason prompted.

"Do they inquire into that on the witness stand, Mr. Mason?"

"They could be asking questions in just about the way that I ask them."

"I see. Then they'd force me to go into it in front of the jury, wouldn't they?"

"Well," Mason said, "it would be up to you."

"I don't want to be a witness," she said.

"You still haven't given me the answer to the question."

She said, with flashing eyes, "I don't think it's any of your damn business," and then after a moment added, with a twinkle, "incompetent, irrelevant, and immaterial to you, Mr. Perry Mason."

He bowed and said, "The objection is well taken, Miss Tooms."

She laughed at that. "You and I," she announced, "could be friends. Listen, you said I had an observing mind. I've had to develop it. I'm crazy about tennis. I like all sports. A girl can't work in an office and get very much time for outdoor recreation."

"That," Mason observed dryly, "is axiomatic."

She said, "I might have an ex-husband somewhere in the background who is paying a small amount of alimony."

"Have you?" Mason asked.

"I thought you said the objection was well taken."

"It was."

"Then I don't need to answer the question."

He shook his head.

She said, "Things don't look so good for Mae Farr, do they?"

"I would say that Hal Anders was in the toughest spot," Mason observed.

"You know, she *could* have been working with him. He could have killed Wentworth right there in the harbor, and he could have taken Wentworth's boat out and set it on the course for Ensenada. She could have tagged along in the cruiser, picked him up, put him ashore at some other dock, and then returned Marley's boat."

"What," Mason asked, "gave you that idea?"

She laughed and said, "Just reading the papers and thinking things over. Naturally, as soon as I read the papers, I appreciated the significance of what I'd seen."

"Did you tell anyone about it?"

She shook her head.

"Why not report to the police?" Mason asked.

"The police?" she said, and shrugged her shoulders.

"Well, why not?"

"Several reasons."

"Such as?"

She said, "I don't want to have to go on the witness stand."

"And, therefore, decided that you'd say absolutely nothing to anyone about what you'd seen?"

She pinched the fold in the leg of her lounging pajamas between her thumb and forefinger and slid her hand down the crease, then sighted along it with a critical eye as though to see if it was absolutely straight.

"Well?" Mason asked.

"Look here," she said abruptly, "I've long ago come to the conclusion that a person can get what he wants out of life, if he wants it badly enough."

"I have heard others advance the same idea," Mason commented.

"Well, I've lived my life according to that theory. I get what I want, but it's not particularly easy. You have to want what you want with every ounce of energy and vitality you possess."

"And so?"

"And so I've learned to be absolutely cold-blooded and selfish," she said, meeting his eyes defiantly.

"Most successful people are selfish," Mason said. "Most strong people are selfish. Here and there, you find the exception which proves the rule. I'm discussing generalities. If you're selfish, don't apologize for it."

"I'm not apologizing."

"Then," Mason said, "I take it you're leading up to something."

"I am."

"Then lead up to it."

"All right. Look here. If I go to the police, I'll have my name in the papers. I'll have to go on the witness stand. They'll have photographs of me. I think I'd photograph rather well—for newspaper purposes. That proposed trip to Ensenada would be magnified and distorted."

"I thought you didn't care for appearances," Mason said.

"I don't, but I do care for reputation."

"So what?"

"So, Mr. Mason, if I go on the witness stand, I'm going to hurt your client. Your client shouldn't want me to go on the witness stand. This man Anders shouldn't want me to go on the witness stand. *You* shouldn't want me to go on the witness stand. *I* don't want to go on the witness stand.

"I would like to take a trip. I know someone who has a yacht. I won't mention any names. That someone and I could start on a cruise to the South Seas. We'd have all kinds of bad luck. The engine would break down. We'd be blown off course, would make a landing at some isolated tropical island, would be out of fuel, would have to repair the mast and sails, and it would be weeks or months before we'd be heard of again."

"Rather a dangerous way to avoid going on the witness stand, isn't it?" Mason asked.

"I don't think so. I'd love it."

"What seems to be holding you back?" Mason inquired.

She said suddenly, "Oh, I see what you mean. You think it's Frank Marley. No, it isn't. Frank has to stay here. This person has a small auxiliary. Marley's boat

could never make a long ocean voyage. It would be fool-
ishness to even try."

"Well, I'll put it another way," Mason said. "What's
holding this other person back?"

"Money," she said.

"Money?"

"Yes—or the lack of it, if you want to put it that
way."

"I see."

"Mr. Mason," she said eagerly, "it wouldn't take very
much money to do the trick, and—in case you have a
conscience—you wouldn't be paying me to stay off the
witness stand. It would be simply a proposition of financ-
ing me on a little trip I've always wanted to take. A
thousand dollars would cover the whole cost."

Mason shook his head.

"Seven-fifty?" she said.

Again Mason shook his head.

"Look, Mr. Mason. I'll do it for five. It would be quite
a job because we'll have to be gone for a long time,
and this other party has certain obligations, but we
could do it for five."

Mason said, "No. It isn't a matter of price."

"What is it?"

"It's a six-letter word," Mason said. "I'm not certain
you'd understand."

"Oh, please, Mr. Mason. You don't know how much it
means to me."

Mason shook his head, got up from the chair, pushed
his hands down deep into his trouser pockets and stood
for a moment lost in thought. Then he started pacing the
room, not the aimless pacing of mental preoccupation,
but a slow, studied tour of inspection along the baseboard of the four walls of the room.

"What is it?" she asked, watching him with apprehensive eyes.

"Just thinking," Mason said.

"You're looking along the floor."

"Am I?"

"Yes."

Mason continued his slow progress around the room.

She walked over to stand at his side. "What is it, Mr. Mason?" she asked. Then, as he didn't answer, she placed a pleading hand on his shoulder. "Look, Mr. Mason. It wouldn't cost you a thing. Harold Anders is rich. He has lots of money and lots of land. I'm a poor girl. Gosh, what he'd have to pay me wouldn't be a drop in the bucket compared to what he'd pay you for defending him."

"I'm not his lawyer," Mason said.

She paused suddenly, thinking that over, then after a moment said, "Oh."

Mason finished his tour of inspection.

"Who is Mr. Anders' lawyer?" she asked.

"I don't know. He's consulted someone up north, someone around North Mesa."

"In North Mesa?"

"Probably in the county seat."

"You don't know his name?"

"No."

She said, "Listen, Mr. Mason, will you do me a favor? As soon as you find out just who is representing him, will you give me a ring and let me know? You could do that much and—and it might amount to the same thing."

Mason said, "Under the circumstances, you'd better read the newspapers and get your information from them."

"All right, I will. Look here, Mr. Mason. I put my cards on the table with you because I had that proposition to make you. You won't take advantage of me, will you?"

"How do you mean?"

"This trip to Ensenada and what I've told you about what I do—how I get my yachting trips?"

Mason said, "When you put your cards on the table, you can't very well expect the other man not to know what you're going to play."

"You wouldn't do that to me, would you?"

"I don't know," Mason said. "It would depend on what you did to me."

"But I'm giving you a fair deal."

Mason raised his voice. "All right, let's hope so. In any event, I won't pay five cents to suppress your testimony. I won't let my client pay five cents."

"You aren't going to tell the police about what I saw?"

Mason said, "Don't worry. I'm not working up a case against the district attorney." He picked up his hat and moved toward the door. "Good-bye, Miss Tooms."

She made a little grimace. "Oh, Mr. Mason, I had hoped you'd be reasonable."

"And do what?"

"You know."

Mason said, "People have different ideas about what's reasonable. It depends somewhat on the viewpoint. Good night."

She raised her eyes to his. "Don't forget, Mr. Mason."

"I won't."

It was as he started down the hall toward the elevator that she called to him. "And don't forget I have an observing mind."

The door closed gently but firmly.

11

MASON FOUND a little hotel two blocks from Hazel Tooms' apartment. He called Paul Drake from the telephone booth. "Hi, Paul," he said. "What's new?"

Drake's voice showed excitement. "Lots of stuff, Perry.

Listen. You were tailed when you left the office. Della tried to get you but was too late. A couple of plain-clothesmen followed that taxicab. Where did you go—any place important?"

"I figured as much," Mason said. "I went to see a witness. She kept making me offers, saying that she would skip out if my clients would give her some money."

"Well?" Drake asked.

Mason said, "About the third time she made the proposition, it sounded awfully fishy to me. I walked around the apartment to see if I could find any evidence of its being bugged."

"Find any?"

"No. They were too smart. A bug is hard to locate, but usually when one is installed on a hurry-up job, a little fine plaster dust will adhere to the baseboard."

"Then you think this witness was planted?"

"No," Mason said slowly, "I don't think she was a plant. I think she's a witness, but she may be trying to buy her way out of something with the police. You know, if they could catch me in a scheme to spirit a witness out of the country, they'd let her get off to a running start, then drag her back with a big fanfare of trumpets, and the fact that I'd tried to get rid of her would raise the devil with my client and with me. Her testimony would automatically become the most important evidence in the case."

"You didn't fall for it?"

"Hell, no!"

Drake said, "I've got those pictures here."

"Have you got an extra gun around there anywhere, Paul?"

"Why, yes."

"One you don't think much of?"

"I have a couple of cheap revolvers that some of my

operatives took away from ambitious lads who played with grown-up toys. Why?"

"How far," Mason asked, "could you throw one?"

"Shucks, I don't know, a hundred feet perhaps."

"Ever tried it?"

"No, of course not."

Mason said, "Better get Della Street, Paul, and meet me at that restaurant where I sometimes eat lunch. Della knows the place. Had anything to eat?"

"Yes, I grabbed a bite."

"Well, I'll take a taxi there, eat something, and be ready to go. I think Della will have had dinner."

"I doubt it," Drake said. "She was all worked up about getting word to you about those shadows. Where are they now, Perry? Did you ditch them?"

"Damned if I know," Mason said. "Probably not. I looked around but didn't spot anyone. However, a man came through the door of the apartment house when I was ringing the bell for this girl's apartment. He may have been one of them."

"What'll that mean, Perry?" Drake asked. "Anything serious?"

"Hell, I don't know," Mason said. "I can't afford to waste time figuring what the other man is going to do. I have to work fast."

Drake said, "I have some hot dope on Eversel."

"What is it?"

"His plane went out and returned twice—once before and once after the rain."

"You're sure?" Mason asked.

"Yes. One of my operatives got the chief gardener of the estate to give him a job as an assistant. It's a steady job. He's on the place, so he can get anything we want."

"Can you call him?" Mason asked.

"No, I can't call him, but he calls me for instructions."

"Okay," Mason said. "I have an idea or two. Get your

stuff together, pick up Della, and meet me at the restaurant. See you there. Good-bye."

He went out to stand in the doorway of the hotel. He saw no one who seemed to be taking any undue interest in his motions.

Mason summoned a taxi and went to the restaurant where he had time for a sandwich, coffee, and piece of pie before Paul Drake joined him.

"Della with you?" Mason asked.

"Yes, sitting outside in the car."

"Has she had anything to eat?"

"She grabbed a sandwich and says she's not hungry now."

"Did you bring that gun?"

"Yes."

Mason said, "Let's get a couple of five-cell flashlights. I want to see how far I can throw that gun."

"Where are you going to do the pitching?" Paul Drake asked.

"Down where Anders did."

Drake surveyed Mason with alarm. "That," he said, "may be dangerous."

"Why?"

"It might not sound good in court."

Mason said, "Love letters don't sound good in court, but people go on writing them just the same."

"Go to it," Drake said. "It's your party. Were you followed here, Perry?"

"I don't think so, but I'm not sure," Mason said. "I went through the usual maneuvers without turning up anybody."

On the way out to the car, Drake said, "My operative out at Eversel's estate certainly had a lucky break. The gardener's a Scot. He's sort of a privileged character, has a little cottage of his own and isn't really classed as one of the servants."

"Where does your operative stay?" Mason asked.

"In a room in the basement."

"Find out anything?"

"Lots. The gardener didn't go on the whoopee party with the servants, although he was supposed to. He's just about as taciturn as a granite rock—unless, like my man, MacGregor, you happen to come from a certain section of Scotland."

They stepped out to the curb. Mason saw Della Street sitting in Drake's automobile, grinned, and said, "Hi, Della."

She said, "Gosh, I was worried about you. I was afraid you were going to walk right into a trap."

Mason said "I may have at that. What did your man find out, Paul?"

Drake slid in behind the wheel. Mason eased in beside him. Della made herself comfortable in the back seat.

"Where to?" Drake asked.

"Down to the place where Anders says he threw the gun," Mason said. "You might see if anyone's on our tail, Paul."

"Okay," Drake said. "Do I get violent about it and let them know we're wise to them?"

Mason thought for a minute, then shook his head and said, "No. Do it casually, Paul. Pretend that we're looking for an address. That'll give you a chance to do a little turning and twisting."

"Okay," Drake said, "but my hunch is they won't try to follow us if they haven't quit already. A wise shadow usually checks out when the man he's after steers a zig-zag course, no matter what the pretext—that is, unless he's told that it doesn't make any difference whether suspect spots him or not."

"Well," Mason said, "you do whatever you can get away with and make it look innocent. What about the gardener at Eversel's?"

Gliding out into traffic, Drake said, "The gardener opened up. It seems that after the servants had left,

Eversel came in with his car. After a while he took his plane, went somewhere, and came back. When he came back, a woman was with him. My operative thinks the gardener knows who it was, but the gardener wouldn't say. Understand, my man had to beat around the bush getting this out of him."

"I understand," Mason said. "Give me what you have, and we'll fill in the blanks."

"Well, Eversel came home with this woman and went directly to a room that Eversel keeps fitted up as a darkroom. It seems he's quite a camera fiend."

"Mrs. Wentworth still with him?" Mason asked.

"The woman, whoever she was."

"Then what happened?"

"Then it started to rain. Eversel went down and warmed up the motor on the plane. About fifteen minutes later, they took off. He was gone nearly all night, came back along toward morning. He came back alone."

Mason said, "Mrs. Wentworth was supposed to have been in San Diego."

"Uh huh," Drake said. "The plane could have taken her down rather easily. I have my San Diego correspondents checking to find out if the plane was seen there."

"Where was Eversel's yacht?"

"Apparently moored in the outer yacht harbor."

"What speed does she turn up?"

"About two knots an hour faster than Wentworth's boat at cruising speed, and she can go about five knots faster."

"Where was Mrs. Wentworth staying in San Diego, Paul?"

"On a yacht with some friends. She also had a room at one of the hotels. You know how it is on a yacht, Perry. You have lots of conveniences, but it's hard to take baths, get beauty appointments, and things like that. Many of the women get a room and spend part of the time there when their yachts are in a city. Sometimes they'll all pitch in and get a room together."

Mason said, "Did you find out anything about where Juanita Wentworth was that night?"

"The people on the yacht said she went to a room at the hotel. As far as the people at the hotel are concerned, they know nothing. If they do know, they aren't making any comments."

"If it came to a pinch, think she could prove that she was in the hotel?"

"She might," Drake said. "I doubt if anyone could prove that she *wasn't*. . . . Well, this looks like a good place, Perry. We'll swing around the block and stop down on one of the side streets, turn the spotlight on a house number or two, then drive on for another block and stop."

"Okay," Mason said, "go to it."

Drake turned the corner, ran two blocks, then turned another corner.

"Oh, oh," Della Street said. "Headlights behind us."

"Don't look around" Mason said. "Paul can watch them in his rear-view mirror."

Drake turned the corner, stopped the car, played the beam of his flashlight over the house numbers, and then moved into slow motion.

The car behind them also turned to the right, came straight toward them, the occupants showing no sign of interest in the car that was parked at the curb.

"Keep your head turned away from it," Mason instructed in a low voice. "Roll your eyes for a quick glance."

He had just finished talking when the other car, which had slowed its speed appreciably, speeded up and swept on past.

Drake looked at the taillight going straight on down the street and said, "I think that's the last we'll see of them, Perry."

"Think they know we're wise?"

"I wouldn't doubt it. Anyhow, they gave me the idea they were signing off."

"Same here," Mason said. "When's that operative down at Eversel's place going to report again?"

"In an hour."

Mason said, "Let's go. I want to perform an experiment with guns, and then I want to be within reaching distance of Eversel's place when your man telephones. He'll telephone directly to the office, Paul?"

"Yes."

Mason said, "Better telephone your office, Paul, and tell them to hold this man on the line when he comes on. We'll want to talk with him."

"Okay, Perry."

Drake started the car once more. They ran down the side street for some fifteen blocks, turned and crossed the main boulevard intersection, then kept on going until they reached another parallel boulevard.

"Try this one," Mason said.

They made the boulevard stop, swung left, and shot into quick speed. Della Street, looking behind through the rear window, said, "No one turned into the boulevard from our street, Paul."

Drake said, "I tell you they've quit. Their instructions were to shadow you as long as you didn't get suspicious. The minute you got suspicious, they were to quit."

Mason said, "Okay, Paul. Show a little speed. Stop at the first store you see that will be selling flashlights. I want to get a couple of five-cell lights."

"I have one pretty good flashlight," Drake said. "It's only three cells, but . . ."

"We'll use that," Mason said, "and also get a couple of bigger ones."

Five minutes later, Drake found a drugstore where he was able to get the flashlights and phone his office. Another fifteen minutes found them driving past the hot-dog stand which Mae Farr had pointed out to Mason.

Mason said, "Take a run down the road half a mile, Paul, turn around and come back. Drive slowly as you go past the place. Let's see if anyone's on guard."

Drake drove down the road, turned the car in a U-turn, swung back, slowed down, and said, "Looks deserted, Perry."

"All right, stop," Mason said. "Pull well over to the side of the road. Shut off your motor. We'll listen and see if we can see or hear anyone over there."

Drake shut off the motor, pushed the lights down to dim, and the trio sat listening for several minutes.

At length Mason said, "Okay, Paul. Nothing ventured, nothing gained. You get out and you, too, Della. We'll wait for a moment when there are no cars passing. I'll throw the gun with my right hand. I'll try and keep the beam of this flashlight on it with my left hand. You folks can each hold a flashlight and try and follow the course taken by the gun."

"What's the idea?" Drake asked. "Trying to show that it would only have hit the high tension pole once out of a thousand times?"

Mason said, "No, that line isn't worth a damn in front of a jury. There's always someone among the twelve who likes to believe that the hand of an all-wise providence betrayed the criminal to his own undoing. Let him get an idea like that through his head, and he becomes a fanatic, feels that if he brings in a not-guilty verdict, he's defying providence. No, Paul, I just want to see how far I can throw the gun."

"Well," Drake said, "here's a good time as soon as that car passes."

"Okay," Mason said, looking up and down the road. "Let's get ready."

He took the gun which Drake gave him, hefted it by the barrel, flexed his arm like a baseball pitcher.

132

A car tore past them at high speed, vanished down the road, the sound of its tires on the pavement a high-pitched snarl.

Mason said, "Okay. Here we go. One . . . two . . . three."

The gun sailed up in the air, Mason's flashlight caught it, followed it, lost it, caught it again. Della Street's flashlight caught it and held it. Drake's light groped uncertainly for a moment, then focused on the moving object.

Together they watched it sail out across the fence over the pasture and down to the ground.

Drake said, "That was a darn good throw, Perry. I might be able to sign you up with the Coast champions —if you could keep away from murders long enough."

Mason said, "Let's go see just where it lit. Take a bearing for direction, Paul. Let's go."

Della said, "How does a lady climb over a barbed-wire fence in the presence of two gentlemen?"

"She doesn't," Mason said. "Ladies are always lifted over."

Della laughed, put her hand on Mason's arm for support when her shoes slipped as they made their way down the steep side of the road, and they crossed the muddy ditch to the barbed-wire fence on the other side. Mason and Drake lifted her clear, swung her over the fence. They held down the top wire, stepped over, and walked across the soft, moist earth.

Mason said, "Don't use your flashlights any more than necessary. When you do, shield them the best you can."

They trudged silently for several seconds, then Drake said, "There it is, Perry, right ahead."

Mason stopped and looked the ground over. "That," he said, "is farther than I'd figured."

"It was a darn good throw," Drake said. "I couldn't do it."

Mason said, "No, but you're not an outdoor man. You

don't live on a cattle ranch, ride horses, and rope cattle. This must be a good ten feet beyond that concrete pipeline."

"It is," Drake said. "What's the idea, Perry?"

Mason said, "Do you know, Paul, it's occurred to me that there are just two places that haven't been searched."

"Where?"

"One of them," Mason said, "was the drainage ditch. That ditch had some water in it. The police neglected to search it right at the start. The newspaperman found the gun there later. The other place the police didn't search is the overflow pipes on this concrete pipeline. There's water in the bottom of those big pipes."

Drake said, "It would have been expecting a lot to throw a gun and have it light ker-*plunk* right in the middle of a pipe. What's more, the police have found the gun with which the murder was committed. So why look for any more guns?"

Mason said, "Because I figure there are some."

"Well, I guess you're the only one who feels that way about it. You want to take a look down those concrete standpipes?"

"Yes."

"Just how?"

Mason said, "I don't know. I think our flashlights will penetrate enough to show whether there's anything like a gun lying at the bottom."

Drake said, "Well, there are only about three pipes that he could possibly have hit. The road makes a swing fifty yards above here. The pipeline continues to run straight."

Mason said, "Let's take a look."

The detective bent over one of the pipes. Mason walked on to the next one. Della Street turned back down the pipeline.

Mason found the big concrete pipe protruding some

four feet above the ground. He leaned over, pushed his flashlight well down into the interior, and switched it on.

The beam of the light, striking the rough, white sides of the pipe, diffused into light-spray which made it hard for Mason to focus his eyes on the place where the main pencil of light entered a body of murky water.

After playing the flashlight around for a minute, he suddenly stepped back and called, in a low voice which however penetrated, "Oh, Paul, take a look at this, will you? Bring Della with you."

Mason stood by the side of the concrete pipe, his lips twisted into a faintly sardonic smile. He could hear the steps of Della Street and the detective approaching through the darkness.

"Here," he said. "Take a look at this."

Della had to raise herself on her tiptoes and prop her elbows against the edge of the pipe. Mason and the detective leaned over. Mason switched on his flashlight.

After a moment Paul Drake said, "I see it down there under the water. By George, it *is* a gun."

Della Street said nothing. Mason looked up to encounter her eyes, troubled and apprehensive.

Mason said, "Well, it looks as though I'm due to get my feet wet."

He removed shoes and socks, rolled up his pants, and said, "I can't get out, Paul, unless you lean over and give me your hand. Let's make sure you can make it."

Drake leaned over and down the side of the concrete.

Della said, "I can hold his legs."

"You may have to at that," Drake said.

Mason said, "I don't want to scratch my bare feet. Ease me down as much as you can, Paul."

He clasped the detective's right forearm, holding it around the wrist with both of his hands. Drake, with

135

his left arm and leg clinging to the edge of the pipe, lowered Mason down into the murky water.

"Brr-r-r-r-r," Mason exclaimed. "This water feels almost freezing."

A moment later he let go his hold, dropped a few inches, then, assuming almost a sitting posture, groped with his hand down in the water.

"Here it is," he said.

He brought up a gun, his bent, right index finger sticking through the trigger guard. Gently he sloshed it back and forth in the water, getting the mud removed from the metal.

Taking his flashlight from his coat pocket and flashing the beam on the gun, he said, "This is a Colt thirty-eight special on a forty-four frame. Okay, Paul, give me a hand up."

Drake said, "Unless you planted that gun sometime this afternoon, this is the damnedest coincidence I ever heard of."

"No coincidence to it," Mason said, as he put the gun into one pocket of his coat and the flashlight in the other. "These pipes are arranged at just about the distance a good strong man would heave a gun. They're not very far apart. At least three of them are within a throwing radius. The pipes are about four and a half or five feet in diameter. Reduce that into square feet, and you'll see that it's not at all unreasonable to suppose the gun would hit one of these pipes—oh, say, once out of five."

Drake stretched down his right arm, braced himself with his left. Mason seized the hanging wrist, and, by the joint efforts of Della Street and the detective, was pulled up to a point where he could climb over the edge of the concrete pipe.

"Gosh," he said, "a guy jumping down there without friends to help him would be up against it."

Gathered around the outside of the pipe, they inspected the gun.

"What are you going to do with it?" asked Drake.

Mason said, "That's the problem." He swung out the cylinder and said, "Six shells, none of them fired."

"Can't you notify the police?" Della asked.

"And have them say I'd planted the gun?"

"You think this is Anders' gun, Perry?" Drake inquired.

"Sure, it's the sort of gun he'd carry. It's the one he threw away."

"Then how did the murder gun get there?"

Mason shrugged his shoulders.

Della started to say something, then checked herself.

Drake said, "Gosh, Perry, there's nothing you *can* do. If you turn this gun in, they'll claim you planted it. If you drop it back in the pipe, you can't get the police to do any more searching. They've found the gun they want, and even if someone did find this gun, they'd claim it had been taken out and planted long after the murder."

Mason took a handkerchief from his pocket and carefully folded it around the gun to dry it off.

Out on the highway a car swerved violently with the sound of screaming tires. Mason, looking musingly at the highway, said, "Now what the devil do you suppose scared *that* driver?"

Della said quietly, "I think there's a car parked without lights, Chief. I had just a glimpse of it when the headlights of that automobile picked it up."

"Right on the highway?" Mason asked.

"No, off to the side, but the driver evidently didn't see it until he was right on top of it, and then got frightened."

Drake said, "Let's get out of here, Perry."

"Just a minute," Mason said. "I want to get the numbers on this gun."

Holding the gun in his handkerchief, he held the flashlight on the numbers and read them off to Della Street, who jotted them down.

Drake said, "We could all of us testify to the finding of the gun."

Mason shook his head. "It wouldn't do a damn bit of good," he said. "Holcomb would still think I'd planted it. Anyway, I'm satisfied in my own mind."

"What are you going to do with the thing, Perry?"

"Drop it back into the pipe," Mason said.

He extended his hand over the opening of the concrete pipe, holding the gun by the trigger guard.

Suddenly a blinding light bathed them with white brilliance, etching their figures against the black background of the night shadows. A voice from the darkness said, "Hold it. Stay just as you are."

Mason remained motionless.

The authoritative voice said, "Get that gun, Jim, before he drops it."

Dim shadowy figures, moving behind the shaft of bright light, converged on the group gathered around the pipe. The beams of individual flashlights crisscrossed to converge upon the motionless figure of Perry Mason. A man ran into the cone-shaped shaft of the light, the glare illuminating his set profile, reflecting from the gold shield which was pinned to his coat. "Don't make a move," he warned.

He grabbed the gun from Mason's hand.

Drake said, "What's the idea?"

Della turned so that her eyes were shielded from the glare. Sergeant Holcomb ran into the area of illumination. "You're under arrest," he said.

Mason said, "What's the charge, Sergeant?"

"Lower that searchlight," Sergeant Holcomb ordered.

The beam of the searchlight dropped so that its glare was not in their eyes.

"Compounding a felony," Sergeant Holcomb said.

"Doing what?" Mason asked.

"Planting evidence."

"We weren't planting anything," Mason said. "We found this gun in the pipe."

"Yeah. I know," Holcomb said.

Mason said, "I'm telling you. Suit yourself, Sergeant. Don't say I haven't warned you."

"You're in a hell of a position to give anyone a warning," Sergeant Holcomb said.

Mason shrugged his shoulders.

"What's that other gun?" Sergeant Holcomb asked Paul Drake.

"A gun we used for an experiment," Drake said. "Mason wanted to see how far he could throw it."

"Give it here," Sergeant Holcomb ordered.

Drake passed over the gun.

"Thought you were pretty smart, didn't you, Mason?" Holcomb said.

Mason glanced across to Sergeant Holcomb's triumphant face. "If the term is relative," he said, "the answer is 'yes.' "

Holcomb said, "None of your wisecracks, Mason. Save those for the judge."

"I will," Mason assured him.

Holcomb said, "Here, boys, put a string around this gun for identification. And keep it separate from the other one until we all get back to headquarters and label them for exhibit."

Mason, propping himself against the water pipe, casually dried his feet with his pocket handkerchief, put on his socks and shoes.

Sergeant Holcomb said, "We figured you'd be down here just as soon as you thought you'd ditched the shadows. We didn't miss it far, did we, Mason?"

Mason said nothing.

Drake said, "Look here. All three of us can testify that that gun was in that pipe lying under the water."

"Sure it was," Holcomb said. "Who put it there? Perry Mason."

Mason finished tying his shoelace, stretched and yawned, then said to Drake, "Well, there's no use sticking around here, Paul."

Sergeant Holcomb said, "I guess you didn't hear me say you were under arrest."

"I heard you," Mason said, "but the words don't mean anything. If you've been watching this place, you saw what happened. You saw me go down inside that pipe and pull out the gun."

"A gun you'd planted," Sergeant Holcomb said.

"Any evidence of that?" Mason asked.

"I don't need any. You were getting ready to drop the gun back down the pipe when we stopped you."

"Too bad you stopped me then," Mason said casually, "if you wanted to make out any sort of a case."

He turned away from Sergeant Holcomb and started toward the road. "Come on, folks, let's go."

For a moment Sergeant Holcomb stood undecided, then he said, "I'll let you go this time, Mason, but you won't get far."

Mason flung back over his shoulder, "I haven't far to go, Sergeant."

Della Street and Paul Drake exchanged glances, then followed the lawyer. A group of officers around the concrete pipe stood still while Mason, Drake, and Della, lighting their way with flashlights, crossed the slippery field in silence.

"Over the fence she goes," Mason said to Drake.

They lifted Della over the fence. Mason and Drake climbed over.

Drake said to Mason, "I don't like this, Perry. I think we should have stuck around. You can't tell what they'll do."

Mason said, "I don't give a damn what they do.

140

When is your man due to telephone in from Eversel's place, Paul?"

"About twenty minutes from now."

"Let's get to a telephone," Mason said.

"You want to go toward Eversel's?" Drake asked.

"Yes," Mason said, "and when your man telephones, tell him that we want to talk with him. We'll drive out to the grounds, and he can arrange to meet us."

They drove silently for several minutes, then Drake said, "Look here, Perry. How much of a spot are we in?"

Mason grinned and said, "We'll get some newspaper notoriety. You can trust Sergeant Holcomb for that."

"And then what?"

"That'll be all," Mason said.

"You mean they won't do anything about planting evidence?"

"We didn't plant any, did we?"

"No, but that isn't going to keep them from trying to do something about it."

Mason said, "Forget it."

Della said to Paul Drake, "Don't you get the sketch, Paul? He knew that those officers were going to be there."

Drake took his eyes from the road to stare at the lawyer. "Did you, Perry?"

"Well," Mason admitted, "when we started out toward the harbor and ditched the follow car, I had an idea Sergeant Holcomb might think we were headed toward that field. I didn't know just what sort of reception he'd plan for us."

"But why stick your head into a lion's mouth?" Drake asked.

"How else would you have gotten the Police to consider the possibility that there was more than one gun?"

"Did you know that gun was there, Perry?"

"I didn't *know* it was there. I thought it *might* be there."

Drake said, "Well, that's a load off my mind. I thought they'd caught you off first base."

"They did," Mason said with a chuckle, "and so we're going to run to second."

"And what'll happen if they throw the ball to second?"

"Then we'll steal third," Mason said.

Drake sighed. "An optimist like you has no business playing baseball," he said, and devoted his attention to driving the car.

Mason consulted his wristwatch from time to time. At length he said, "How about this little roadhouse café, Paul? It looks as though they'd have a telephone."

Drake slowed the car and swung it from the highway to the graveled driveway beneath the red glare of the neon sign. "Yes," he said, "they have a public phone. There's a sign."

Mason turned to Della in the back seat. "How about a bowl of hot soup, Della?" he asked.

"It would go fine," she admitted.

Mason said, "Let's eat. If you get your man on the phone, Paul, hold him on the line, find out who's home down at the estate."

"Okay," Drake said.

They entered the restaurant, seated themselves at a table for four, and ordered hot soup and coffee. Paul Drake had a hamburger in addition.

Mason grinned and said, "Eating our dinner on the progressive installment plan."

"I'm loading up with grub," Drake admitted, "on the theory that jail fodder won't agree with me."

"They say you get accustomed to it after a while," Mason observed cheerfully.

"Yes, I know. The first eight or ten years are the hardest."

When Drake was halfway through his hamburger, Mason, consulting his wristwatch, said, "Well, Paul, just to be safe, you'd better get on the telephone and hold the line to your office."

Drake nodded, scraped back his chair, entered the telephone booth, and remained closeted for some three minutes, then opened the door and beckoned to Mason.

The lawyer crossed over to him.

"My man's on the line," Drake said. "The servants are out again. The gardener's gone to bed. My man says we can drive out and he'll meet us at the gates."

"You know the way?" Mason asked.

"Yes."

Mason said, "Okay, let's go."

"It'll take us about twenty minutes to get out there," Drake said into the telephone. "You'd better be there waiting."

He hung up the telephone and turned to Mason. "Of course, Perry," he said, "if anything happens and our man gets caught, it spoils the perfectly swell connection. There's not one chance in a thousand I could get another operative planted in time to do us any good."

"I know," Mason said, "but it's a chance I have to take. Fortunately I like to take chances."

Drake said lugubriously, "I'll say you do."

Mason paid the check. When they were once more on the road, Drake asked, "Exactly what are your plans, Perry? Not that I want to interfere, but in case you expect police officers to be there, I'd like to know about it in advance. My heart won't stand many more of those little surprises."

"Oh, this is all right," Mason said cheerfully. "I don't think the officers will follow us any more tonight. The worst we can expect now is to be arrested for burglary."

"Perry!" Drake exclaimed. "You're not going to try to get in that house?"

"I am if I can make it," Mason said.

"Good Lord, why?"

Mason said, "We've overlooked one of the most significant things in the entire case."

"What do you mean, Perry?"

"No one heard the shot."

"Well, what if they didn't? The man was shot. His body shows that, and Mae Farr's statement shows it."

Mason said, "Did it ever occur to you, Paul, that if the shot was fired just at the moment when Hal Anders was dunking in the waters of the bay, it was timed to a split second?"

"Well, it was, wasn't it?"

Mason said, "I don't think so. I don't think there was any shot."

Drake slapped on the brakes so that he could turn to stare incredulously at the lawyer without wrecking the car. "You don't what?" he exclaimed.

"Don't think there was any shot," Mason said.

"Then Mae Farr is lying."

"Not necessarily."

"What do you think happened?"

Mason said, "I'll tell you more about that when I've indulged in a little high-class housebreaking."

Drake groaned and said, "Gosh, Perry, I should have known better."

"*You* don't need to go any farther than the gate," Mason said.

"That's far enough," Drake said, and then, after a moment, added, "it's too damn far."

Mason settled back against the cushions, his eyes staring steadily through the windshield at the lighted ribbon of highway which flowed smoothly toward them. Della Street, in the back seat, kept her own counsel, glancing from time to time at the back of Mason's head, studying the set of his shoulders, studying what she could see of the angle of his jaw. Drake, driving the automobile carefully, was given to periods of contemplation during which he would slow the car appreciably, then, catching himself, would push the speedometer needle up another ten or fifteen miles an hour.

Mason gave no sign that he noticed the irregularities of the driving, and Della surrounded herself with an observant, self-effacing silence.

Drake turned to the right from the main highway, drove several miles, then turned left, following a road which snaked its way up the side of a sharp headland. To the left could be seen the glittering lights of a city and roads studded with automobile headlights. To the right, occasional glimpses of moonlit water finally resolved themselves into a magnificent view of the ocean as the road straightened out on the relatively level ground at the top of the headland.

Drake slowed the car until it was running at a scant twenty-five miles an hour. He said, "There's a turnoff right around here someplace. It—" He interrupted himself to swing the wheel sharply to the left, and the car climbed a short pitch to disclose the gables of a house silhouetted against the sky, a long sweep of hedge, and, after a few moments, in front of the headlights the forbidding barrier of locked iron gates crossing a driveway.

Drake switched off the headlights, turned on the dome light, and said, "Well, here we are."

"Your man's supposed to be here?" Mason asked.

"Yes," Drake said. "Here he is now."

A lighted cigarette glowed as a red coal in the darkness. A moment later a man in rough clothes and with a trace of a Scottish accent said, "You're a bit late."

"The coast all clear?" Drake asked.

"Yes."

Mason took a good look at the man's face, then switched out the dome light as Drake introduced Della Street and the lawyer.

"Exactly what was it you wanted to know?" the man asked.

Mason said quietly, "I want to get in the house, Mac-Gregor."

There was a moment's stiff, uncomfortable silence, then the operative said, "I'm afraid that's going to be a pretty tough order."

"How tough?" Mason asked.

"Plenty tough. Old Angus goes to bed early, but he always reads for an hour or two before he turns out the light. He's a light sleeper."

"Where does he sleep?"

"In a cottage down near the hangar."

"You have a key to the gate?" Mason asked.

"Gosh, no. I'm just an assistant to the gardener. I sleep in a cubbyhole in the basement."

"The door from the basement to the other part of the house unlocked?" Mason asked.

"I could get in. Of course, I'd be fired if I were caught. Then I could either produce my credentials and show I was a private detective on a job, or be sent to jail as a burglar."

"Do you know how long they're going to be gone?"

"The servants won't be back until one or two o'clock. The chauffeur took them to see a picture show in town. God knows when Eversel will show up."

"Doesn't he usually send the servants away when he plans on spending the night elsewhere?"

"He didn't the other night," MacGregor said. "He sent them away to get rid of them."

Mason grinned and said, "Well, let's take a chance."

"You can't leave the car there," MacGregor said, "and I can't get it through the gates. You'll have to drive it back down to the main road and park it."

"I'll take it down," Drake said.

"And stay in it?" Mason asked.

Drake took a deep breath. "Hell, no, Perry," he said.

"I'll stay with you. I don't want to, but you may need my moral support."

Mason glanced inquiringly at Della Street. By way of answer, she opened the door and slipped out of the car to stand by the driveway. "We'll wait for you here, Paul," she said.

Mason said, "Look here, Della. I don't know just what I'm getting into. This may be embarrassing, and it may be dangerous."

"I know," she said quietly, in a tone which completely disposed of the discussion.

Drake slipped the car into reverse. Mason joined Della Street at the driveway, quietly closed the door. "Don't make any more noise than necessary, Paul," he said.

"It's all right," MacGregor told him. "Lots of cars come up here on moonlit nights—not an awful lot, but enough so Angus gets accustomed to hearing them turn back when they come to the locked gates."

Abruptly Mason signaled Paul Drake, walked over to stand near the front left-hand window of the car. "On second thought, Paul," he said, "I think you'd better stay with the car, and you'd better take Della with you."

Della Street quietly shook her head.

"Why not?" Mason asked.

"You may need a witness," she said. "I'm going to stay with you."

Mason said to Drake, "Go back to the main highway, drive about three hundred yards up the road, stop the car, turn out the lights, and wait until you hear from me. If things go all right, I'll join you inside of half an hour. If, at the end of half an hour, you haven't heard from me, beat it back to town."

"If I can help, Perry," the detective said, "I want to. . . ."

"No," Mason told him. "Go on. Beat it. I don't know just what we're getting into. MacGregor's here. He can stand by if it comes to a showdown. You'd better keep on the sidelines, Paul, and get started. Time's precious."

"Okay," Drake said, "thirty minutes," and drove away.

Mason turned to MacGregor. "Let's go," he said.

"We'll work through an opening in the hedge down here about twenty yards," he said. "I'll lead the way."

Casting black, grotesque shadows in the moonlight, the three moved quietly along the hedge. MacGregor led the way through the opening. Inside the grounds, he paused to listen, then whispered, "Just where do you want to go?"

"The room that Eversel went to when he returned to the house," Mason said. "Paul Drake told me it was a darkroom."

"It is. It wasn't built as a darkroom, but it's been fixed over. He has a lot of equipment there, does quite a bit of amateur photography."

"Let's go," Mason said.

"Do you want me to take you all the way up?"

"Yes."

MacGregor said, "Be as quiet as possible. If we use flashlights, cover them with your hand and let as much light as you need work out through your spread fingers. Angus might see lights shining on the windows."

"All right," Mason said. "Let's go."

They crossed the moonlit yard, entered a basement door. MacGregor led the way across the cement floor to a flight of stairs. The door at the head of the stairs was unlocked. They entered a back hallway, passed through a kitchen, and reached a flight of stairs near the back of the house. MacGregor piloted them to an upper corridor and down the corridor to the door. "That," he said, "is the room. Don't turn on any lights."

"We won't," Mason promised.

"Where," MacGregor asked, "do you want me?"

"Someplace on the lower floor," Mason said, "Where you can keep watch but can manage to get back to your room in case anything happens. If anyone drives through the gate, slam the nearest door, and slam it hard, then go back to your room. Keep your ears open. If you hear any commotion, come running. Keep in the character of a servant who has been asleep, was wakened by the commotion, and is loyal to his employer, unless I give you a signal. In that case, come out in the open and take orders from me."

"Okay," MacGregor said quietly. "I'll slam that kitchen door. You can hear that from here if you are listening."

"We'll listen," Mason said.

MacGregor retraced his steps down the hallway. Mason turned the knob of the door and entered the room.

It had evidently been a small bedroom at one time. Now it had been completely done over. The windows were darkened. A battery of light switches led to safelights, enlarging cameras, wired printing boxes, and electrical washers. Shelves were well filled with photographic supplies. A long sink ran the entire length of the room, divided into various tanks for developing, printing, and washing. A long shelf held graduates and photographic chemicals.

Mason said quietly, "I think we can turn on a light here, Della. The room is lightproof."

He experimented with the switches, finally located one which controlled a shielded white light.

"What," she asked, "are you looking for, Chief?"

Mason said, "I think they came here to develop a photograph. After that photograph was developed, it was probably printed in an enlarging camera. We'll look around and see what we can find."

Della Street said, "Here is a file of negatives, Chief."

"How are they listed?" Mason asked. "By dates or subjects?"

"Subjects," she said, "alphabetical order."

Mason said, "This room is too darned orderly to be a good darkroom. Look around for a wastebasket, Della.

Hang it, it doesn't look as though the place had been used for a month, and yet they must have developed a picture here."

Della said, "You don't think Eversel killed him, do you?"

"I don't know," Mason said.

"I've been wondering about that Farr woman," she said. "Do you believe her story, Chief?"

Mason said, "There's no particular reason why I should. She first came to the office with a lie which she had ingeniously worked out—but she's our client, Della. You can't keep clients from lying, but that doesn't relieve you of your responsibility to see they get a square deal."

"Do you think she . . ."

"That she what?" Mason asked as her voice trailed away into silence.

"Oh, I don't know," Della said. "Forget it. We'll see what we can find here. I can talk about Mae Farr later."

Mason said, "We're licked before we start. Hang it, I never saw such an orderly darkroom."

"We might try running through those negative files," she said.

"Yes, we could," Mason agreed dubiously. "I don't think we'd get anywhere."

"What's that big thing that looks like a toy freight car?" Della Street asked.

"Horizontal enlarging camera," Mason said, "nine-inch condensers, takes up to a five-by-seven negative. That screen over there on the track holds the enlarging paper. Let's find the switch for that enlarger, Della. I want to see about how much of a blowup there was on the last negative in there."

Mason clicked switches near the work shelf, turning on first a red light in a printing box, then a white light then, on his third attempt, clicking the huge bulb of the enlarger into light.

Della Street gave a quick, involuntary gasp.

On the white surface of the easel which held the enlarging paper was thrown the image of an enlarged negative, held in the big enlarging camera. Save for the fact that blacks and whites were reversed, it was as though they stood looking down through the skylight of a yacht into a cabin beneath.

A man, with his face half turned as though he had twisted it suddenly to look upward, was struggling with a woman whose face was concealed from the camera. Much of her body was shielded by the man's body. Her arms and legs showed in arrested motion as though the figures had suddenly been frozen into immobility.

Mason said, "That's it, Della."

"I don't understand, Chief."

Mason said, "Wentworth wasn't shot when he was struggling with Mae Farr. What she saw wasn't the flash of a shot, but the flash of a bulb that was synchronized with the shutter of a camera. Those flash bulbs are instantaneous, just a quick burst of light synchronized to the fraction of a second with a camera shutter."

"Then you mean . . ."

"That Eversel took that photograph," Mason said. "You can figure for whom he took it and what he wanted with it."

"And that's why no one heard the shot?"

"Yes."

"Did you know that in advance, Chief?"

"I suspected it," Mason said. "Gosh, I'd like to mix up some developer, put in a sheet of bromide paper, and pull a print of that negative. We could—"

His words were interrupted by the reverberating boom of a slamming door on the lower floor.

Mason looked at Della Street. "In case you don't know it," he said quietly, "this is a felony."

"Of course I know it," she said. "What do you think I've been working in a law office for?"

Mason grinned, pulled up the slide in the enlarging camera, took out the negative holder, removed the negative, and slipped it in his pocket. He switched out the lights and said, "Come on. Let's go."

They ran on tiptoe down the corridor to the back stairs, down the back stairs and through the kitchen to the basement.

MacGregor was waiting for them at the foot of the stairs. "Eversel just drove into the garage," he said quietly.

"Can you get Miss Street out of the grounds?" Mason asked.

"I don't know," MacGregor said. "I can if something occupies his attention. If he happens to be looking out of the window, we're sunk—it's moonlight, you know."

Mason slipped the negative from his pocket. "Let me have your purse, Della."

She gave him her purse. "Think you know what to do with this?" he asked.

"The thing you said you'd like to do up there?"

"Yes. You and Paul Drake beat it. Get that done on the largest scale possible. I'll join you in town."

"What are you going to do?" she asked.

"Pay a social call," he said. "I'll get back."

Mason nodded to MacGregor.

MacGregor let them out of the basement door. Mason walked quietly around the house. MacGregor waited for his signal to cross the yard.

Lights blazed on in the front of the house. Mason, walking around the corner, signaled MacGregor, climbed the front steps, and rang the bell.

For a moment there was no response, then Mason heard the sound of quick steps in the hallway. He stepped back a few paces to look out across the moonlit yard. He glimpsed two fleeting shadows as MacGregor and Della Street made a dash for the break in the hedge. He glanced back toward the ocean. In a low,

152

white building at the far end of the garage he saw lights come on, then go off. A moment later he heard the sound of a door rolling back on a steel track.

Abruptly the porch light flooded him with brilliance. A wicket in the front door swung back. Mason was conscious of a pair of intense eyes staring steadily at him. A voice, ominously calm, said, "Who are you and what do you want?"

"My name's Mason," the lawyer said. "I want to talk with you."

"Are you Perry Mason, the lawyer?" .

"Yes."

"What do you want to talk with me about?"

"About Penn Wentworth."

"I don't care to discuss him with you."

Mason said, "I think you do."

"Well, I don't," the voice said. "This is private property. I don't allow trespassers. I'll give you thirty seconds to get started for the gate. At the end of that time, I'll telephone the police."

The lights on the porch switched out. After a moment the lights in the front of the house went out. Mason was left standing on the front porch in the moonlight.

"Very well," Mason said. He turned, walked down the front steps, but instead of turning to the right toward the gate, turned to the left and strode rapidly toward the hangar.

He was almost at the door of the hangar when he heard the slam of a door in the house behind him and running steps on the graveled walk.

Mason entered the hangar. His flashlight explored the interior, showed a trim, white amphibian plane. Seated in the cabin was a beautiful, olive-skinned woman with dark eyes.

Mason climbed up on the step of the plane and opened the cabin door.

The woman's voice said reproachfully, "You blinded me with that flashlight, dear."

Mason entered the cabin. "I'm sorry, Mrs Wentworth," he said.

At the sound of his voice, she stiffened to attention. Mason saw her lips twitch with emotion. The cabin door jerked open, and the voice of Eversel behind him said, "Get the hell out of here."

Mason calmly sat down in one of the seats.

Eversel said, "Get the hell out."

Juanita Wentworth switched on the lights in the plane, illuminating the cabin, showing Eversel, a bronzed, young giant with reddish-brown, excitable eyes, holding a gun in his right hand.

Mason said, "Better put away the gun, Eversel. Don't you think we've had enough gun play?"

Eversel said, "This is my property. I'm ordering you out and off. If you don't go, I'll treat you as I would any other trespasser."

"I wouldn't advise you to," Mason said. "You're in deep enough already. A witness has identified you as the man who climbed aboard Wentworth's yacht just before the shooting."

He settled back in the seat.

"That's a lie," Eversel said.

Mason shrugged his shoulders.

Juanita Wentworth said, "Please, Sidney—no trouble."

After a moment Eversel asked, "What do you want?"

"A complete statement," Mason said, "admitting that you were the one who boarded the *Pennwent* while Mae Farr was struggling with Wentworth in the cabin."

"I wasn't there," Eversel said.

Mason arched his eyebrows. "After that, you took this airplane and flew to San Diego."

"What if I did? This is a private plane. I go where I damn please."

An amphibian, I notice," Mason said casually. "While

you were flying to San Diego, did you, perhaps, happen to fly over the *Pennwent* and look down into the lighted interior of the cabin?"

"What the devil are you talking about?"

"Just asking questions," Mason said.

"Don't do it. It isn't healthy."

Mason said conversationally, "Do you know, Eversel, I have a peculiar idea about what happened aboard that yacht. You're quite an amateur photographer. It's a funny thing about that shot. No one heard it."

"Well, what's strange about that?" Eversel asked belligerently. "People in the other boats were making whoopee. If they heard a noise, they'd take it as the backfire of a truck or a boat engine."

Mason said, "Do you know, Eversel, I was wondering if it couldn't have been a flashlight bulb that Mae Farr thought was a shot. Wentworth knew he was trapped as soon as the picture was taken. He ran back to the after cabin and held the door tightly shut while he was getting into his clothes. He thought perhaps it was a raid."

Eversel said, "I suppose you'd like to cook up some cock-and-bull story like that in order to get your client, Mae Farr, acquitted of murder."

"She's a little adventuress," Mrs. Wentworth said.

"It was just an idea I had," Mason observed almost apologetically.

"Well, it's an idea that didn't pan out," Eversel said sharply, "and if you make any insinuations like that in court, I'll sue you for slander."

"Of course," Mason went on conversationally, "you hoped that as soon as Wentworth realized the full import of what had happened, he would decide to get in touch with his estranged wife and meet her terms on a property settlement. He knew that photograph would put him in rather a bad light."

"You're crazy," Eversel said.

"You and Mrs. Wentworth wanted to get married," Mason said. "You'd been just a little too eager. Wentworth wouldn't let his wife have an uncontested divorce. You were pretty desperate. You couldn't afford to have your name dragged into a scandal."

"I tell you you're crazy."

Mason went on calmly, "I don't think it was only a question of money. It was probably also a question of jealousy on Wentworth's part. He was fascinated by the woman he had married and who had grown to despise him." The lawyer turned to Mrs. Wentworth and made a little bow. "Seeing Mrs. Wentworth, one can well appreciate how he felt."

Eversel said, "You're not only crazy, but you're insulting. By God, I won't stand for it."

Mason said, "The preliminary hearing is tomorrow morning. Through an understanding with the Justice of the Peace, witnesses whom I think important are subpoenaed."

"Juanita is going to be there," Eversel said.

"So I understand," Mason observed, taking a folded subpoena from his pocket and extending it to Eversel, "and so are you, Eversel."

Eversel dashed the subpoena from the lawyer's hand to the floor. "Not by a damn sight," he said.

Mason shrugged his shoulders and said, "Suit yourself. You can figure whether it's better for you to be there and answer routine questions, or to make yourself conspicuous by your absence and force the Justice to take proceedings to enforce your attendance."

"This is outrageous," Eversel stormed. "It's the work of a shyster criminal lawyer."

Mrs. Wentworth said, "Let me talk with him, Sidney. Please," and then to Perry Mason, "What is it you want, Mr. Mason?"

"I want a square deal for my client," Mason said. "I want you to attend that preliminary hearing and tell the truth."

"What do you mean by the truth?"

"That it wasn't a shot which was fired when Mae Farr was aboard the yacht, it was the taking of a flashlight photograph."

"By whom?" Mrs. Wentworth asked.

Eversel said, "Juanita, don't—"

"Please, Sidney," she interrupted.

Mason said, "By Eversel."

She said, "Mr. Eversel holds several important positions. He's on the board of directors of a bank, a trust company, and other important corporations. He simply can't afford to have any scandal connected with his name."

"Taking a picture doesn't necessarily mean a scandal," Mason said.

"It would in this instance."

"Was fear of scandal," Mason asked, "the hold that Wentworth had over you?"

She met his eyes steadily and said, "Yes."

"And what were you holding out for?"

She said calmly, "Money for my parents. Sidney offered . . . I could have secured it elsewhere, but I was just as obstinate as Penn was. My parents lived on a large hacienda in Mexico. The government took their land and gave it to the peons. They were impoverished. It was only fair that Penn should make some financial settlement. He took an unfair advantage by threatening to drag Sidney's name into the case. I knew Sidney couldn't afford to have the publicity, and Penn knew it too. Penn threatened to sue Sidney for alienation of affections. I knew how to handle Penn. There was only one way. I had to fight him and master him. Otherwise, there would never have been any peace for us."

"How about Eversel?" Mason asked Mrs. Wentworth. "How did he feel about it?"

"He was impulsive," she said. "He was . . ."

157

"Juanita, please don't drag me into this," Eversel said. "He's a shrewd lawyer, and he's just trapping you."

"The truth can't hurt us," she said, and then added, after a significant moment, "now."

"Were you," Mason asked, "glad that your husband was killed?"

"I am not glad to have anyone killed."

"You were relieved?"

She met his eyes and said, "Naturally. It was a shock to me of course. There was much about Penn that was good, and a lot more that was all bad. He desired to dominate people. He wanted to get them in his clutches and in his power. He was a brute—particularly as far as women are concerned."

Mason said, "Well, there's your subpoena, Eversel. You can't say I didn't give you a chance to play fair. If you're going anywhere, you can drop me at an airport where I can pick up a car, and," Mason added with a smile, "when I say drop me, I use the term figuratively."

Eversel said, "To hell with you. You can go back the way you came."

Mason said, "My friends have left. I thought I might have to wait all night to serve the subpoena."

Eversel eyed him suspiciously.

Mrs. Wentworth said, "Please, Sidney. We could leave him in Los Angeles. You don't want to go away and leave him here, do you?"

That idea appeared suddenly disquieting to Eversel.

"Please," Juanita Wentworth asked, flashing him a glance from her limpid, dark eyes. "This is once, Sidney, when I think I know best."

Eversel hesitated a moment, then shoved his gun into a hip pocket, moved over to the pilot's seat in the plane, fastened the seat belt in sulky silence, and oparated the starting mechanism which sent the motor roaring into life. He taxied out to the level field and sat grimly silent while he warmed up the motor of the plane.

Mrs. Wentworth, raising her voice so it could be heard above the sound of the motor, said, "Don't you think, Mr. Mason, it would be better for your client to tell the truth and face the consequences instead of trying to drag us into it?"

Mason, pushing his hands down deep in his trouser pockets, sunk his chin on his chest and stared moodily at the floor of the plane. "That," he said musingly, "is something that's been running through my own mind."

12

■

DAYLIGHT FOUND Mason sitting in the narrow confines of Paul Drake's private office, studying huge, glossy paper enlargements with a magnifying glass.

Drake, seated across the desk, chewed gum nervously. His eyes surveyed the lawyer speculatively. "That," he said, "was the biggest enlargement we could make and still keep any detail in the print. As it is, you'll notice it shows considerable grain. The negative was wire-sharp and fine-grained, but we've blown it up to a point where it commences to get fuzzy. Each one of those prints represents only a quarter of the negative."

"I understand," Mason said, not looking up, but continuing his patient search with the magnifying glass.

"And this other one, the one my pals slipped me," Drake said, "is an eleven-by-fourteen enlargement, from the negative taken after the *Pennwent* was brought into port. I was lucky to get that print. I can get bigger enlargements, but it will take time and a little manipulation."

"Time," Mason said, "is the one thing we haven't got. That preliminary hearing is called for ten o'clock this morning."

"Exactly what," Drake asked, "are you looking for, Perry?"

Mason said, "I'm looking for a lucky break."

"What do you mean?"

"I'm hoping to find something in one photograph which isn't in the other."

"You mean the figures, a person . . ."

"No," Mason said, "some significant difference in the furniture. For instance, look at this cigarette tray. In the picture Eversel took, it has half a dozen cigarette stubs on it. In this picture taken after the body was discovered, there are only two."

"Well?" Drake asked. "What's wrong with that?"

Mason shook his head. "A person committing a murder," he said, "doesn't bother to tidy up the place and empty the ashtrays. If he should do that for any reason, he doesn't stick around to smoke two cigarettes."

Drake frowned. "Exactly what are you getting at, Perry?" he asked.

Mason said, "I'm darned if I know exactly, Paul, but I'm working on the theory of elimination. I'd like to find something to substantiate my idea. If I could— Hello, what's this?"

His magnifying glass remained stationary over a section of one of the enlargements.

Outside, the first rays of sunlight tinted the tops of the office buildings, made the electric light in Drake's office seem artificial and unreal. The morning light, pouring through the window, showed Mason's skin oily with fatigue, brought into prominence the tips of stubble which had grown out on his chin during the last twenty-four hours.

"What is it?" Drake asked.

Mason passed the photograph across to him, indicated a section with his finger, and said, "Take a look, Paul."

Drake studied it through the magnifying glass and

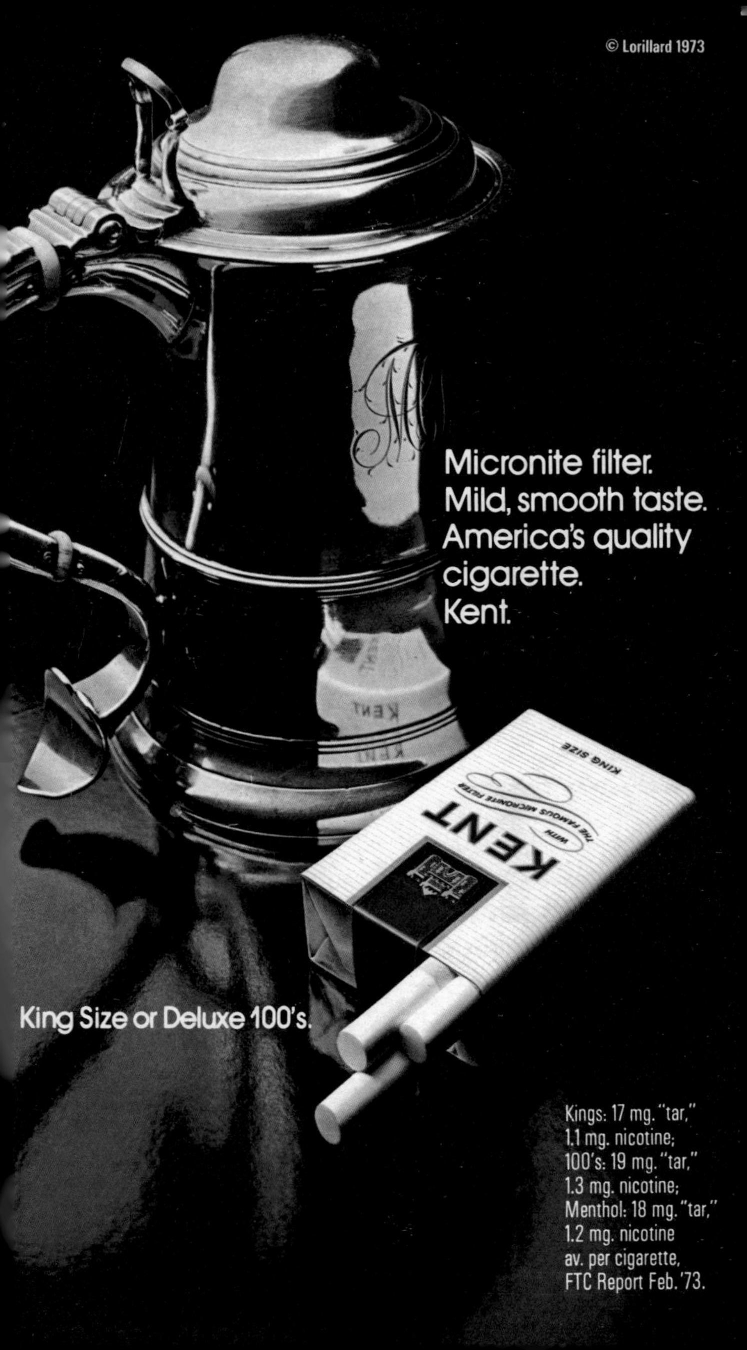
© Lorillard 1973
Micronite filter.
Mild, smooth taste.
America's quality
cigarette.
Kent.
KING SIZE
WITH
THE FAMOUS MICRONITE FILTER
KENT
King Size or Deluxe 100's.
Kings: 17 mg. "tar,"
1.1 mg. nicotine;
100's: 19 mg. "tar,"
1.3 mg. nicotine;
Menthol: 18 mg. "tar,"
1.2 mg. nicotine
av. per cigarette,
FTC Report Feb. '73.

Try the crisp, clean taste of Kent Menthol.

The only Menthol with the famous Micronite filter.

Warning: The Surgeon General Has Determined That Cigarette Smoking Is Dangerous to Your Health said, "Gosh, Perry, it doesn't look like anything to me. It's something round in a case, some kind of a rare coin, I suppose. Wentworth, you know, was quite a collector."

"Uh huh," Mason said. "Let's assume that it is a coin. It isn't so much what the object is as where it went. You'll notice that it doesn't appear in this other photograph, yet it was up on the shelf, and there's something else across the top of that case."

"It looks like a cartridge," Drake said, studying it carefully.

"It does," Mason said, "but I don't think it is a cartridge. Remember, Paul, this picture was taken by a flashlight which makes the lighting rather harsh, and we've enlarged it from rather a small negative. Even so, that could hardly be a revolver cartridge. It would have to be a rifle cartridge, judging from its length."

"Well, why not?" Drake asked.

"The modern rifle," Mason said, "uses a bottleneck cartridge. This is straight across like a revolver shell."

"Couldn't a revolver cartridge be that long?" Drake asked.

"Yes," Mason said, "I guess it could, but—that's rather a big coin, Paul. I wish we could make out some of the details on it."

"You can only get a line here and there," Drake said, "not enough to tell what kind of a coin it is."

Mason narrowed his eyes. "That coin," he said, "must mean something. One thing's certain, Paul. Wentworth wasn't killed at the time it's been generally assumed the shot was fired. He had an opportunity to dress, empty the ashtray, cast loose the lines, start the motor, and put out to sea."

Drake shook his head. "Someone else did that for him, Perry. You can't figure a man being killed on the high seas on a yacht without anyone else being around— not without some evidences of a struggle. A man certainly isn't going to let someone else board his yacht, and . . ."

"Not strangers," Mason said. "A friend might be different."

"Well," Drake said, "even supposing you're right, I don't see what this coin has to do with it particularly."

Mason said, "I'd like to have the *Pennwent* searched from stem to stern to see if we can find that coin."

"It's been gone over with a fine-tooth comb for fingerprints and everything else," Drake said. "The Homicide Bureau of the Police Department has inventories of everything that was found. I can find out if that coin was located."

"It should be a cinch," Mason said, "because it's evidently in a case with a hinged cover. That would mean it's a valuable coin. You can get just a hint of the design, Paul. There's something running across it, a band of crisscross lines."

"Uh huh," Drake said, "probably some sort of a coat of arms."

"It might give us a clue," Mason said thoughtfully, "if we could—"

There was a knock at the door of the office. Drake called, "Come in."

One of his operatives opened the door. "Want to see the papers?" he asked. "There's a lot in there about—about Mr. Mason."

Mason straightened from a contemplation of the photograph. "It'll be a change for my eyes," he said. "What do they say about me?"

"Darn near everything," the operative said with a grin. "It seems you're guilty of just about everything except murder, including bribing a witness to leave the country."

"Bribing a witness?" Mason asked.

"Yes, a girl named Hazel Tooms. It's the theory of the police that someone who wanted her out of the way gave her five hundred dollars to make a trip out of the country. She admitted that much to officers when they served her with a subpoena."

"Mention my name?" Mason asked.

"Not in so many words," the operative said.

Mason spread the paper out on the desk and read in headlines: "OFFICERS CLAIM LAWYER CAUGHT RED-HANDED —POLICE CLAIM PROMINENT ATTORNEY APPREHENDED PLANTING GUN."

Mason turned to Paul Drake with a grin. "Well, Paul," he said, "looks like we're in the news."

Drake placed his extended forefinger on a paragraph midway down the article. "Notice this," he said. " 'Grand jury subpoenas have been issued and will be served sometime today. Police have insisted that the grand jury make a sweeping investigation into the activities of a lawyer whose methods have been noted for dramatic originality rather than a strict adherence to conventional routine. It is rumored that a detective agency which subsists largely on work furnished by the attorney in question will be the subject of a sweeping investigation. If criminal charges are not brought, police intimate that they will at least take steps to prevent a renewal of the agency's license.' "

Mason grinned again at Paul Drake. "How about a little breakfast, Paul?"

Drake said, "Five minutes ago, it would have sounded swell. Right now, I'd have to choke the food down. Gosh, Perry, I hope you know the answer to *this* one."

Mason said, "I think we have enough facts to go on, Paul. What we need right now is a chance to do a little thinking. I'm going to a Turkish bath, get a shave, some breakfast, and I'll meet you at the preliminary hearing."

"What'll happen there?" Drake asked.

Mason said, "One thing about the justice of the peace, Paul. Emil Scanlon is fair. He doesn't like to have cases tried in the newspapers. In view of these accusations, he'll give me every chance to examine witnesses."

"What'll he do with the district attorney?" Drake asked.

"Give him the same chance," Mason said.

Drake ran his fingers through his hair. "And I," he announced mournfully, "am a witness. I'll have you both on my neck."

Emil Scanlon was a unique Justice of the Peace with an appreciation of the dramatic, a keen sense of humor, and a desire to see justice done at all costs. His basic philosophy of life made him as bigheartedly sympathetic with the living as he was scientifically detached with the dead. Taking his role of office conscientiously, he felt himself the representative of both the living and the dead.

Scanlon's first career was that of a professional baseball player of no mean ability who retired to Southern California after an injury shortened his playing days in the early twenties. Elected justice of the peace the first time he ran, he was "grandfathered" into office when California substituted municipal judges for justices of the peace in the larger cities; and even though he had no former legal background or even a high school education, the new law permitted him to be re-elected to the office of justice of the peace year after year to the consternation of a succession of district attorneys and impatient young law school graduates whetting their teeth as defense attorneys.

Scanlon watched Mae Farr as she sat in whispered consultation with Perry Mason and decided that she was far from the cold-blooded killer the district attorney's office claimed. His knowledge of Perry Mason was founded upon various personal contacts, dramatic preliminary hearings when Mason, using a quick wit, keen logic, and unconventional methods, had sprinted first across the tape as a spectacular winner from a position hopelessly behind the field.

There was nothing in Emil Scanlon's voice or face to reflect the determination which crystallized in his mind that, even if the hearing took all night, he was going to see that the various parties had a square shake.

Mae Farr whispered her confession to Perry Mason. "I gave you a raw deal," she said. "I lied to you when I first came to your office and I've been lying to you ever since. When you didn't find Hal's gun there where he'd thrown it over the fence, I became convinced that he'd doubled back, picked up the gun, and gone down to take the *Pennwent* out to sea and sink it, taking the chance of rowing back in the little skiff Wentworth kept aboard.

"I doubled back and took Marley's cruiser and went out to pick him up."

"Find him?" Mason asked.

"No," she said. "I didn't search very long because I became convinced the Coast Guard had been notified of the killing and was looking for me."

"What made you think that?"

"A Coast Guard airplane flew over me, circled three or four times, and then went on out to sea."

"How do you know it was a Coast Guard plane?"

She thought for a moment, and said, "I don't know. I presumed it was. What other flyer would have taken such an unusual interest in a yacht? And that Tooms woman saw me when I came back with Marley's boat, and I understand Marley had a fingerprint expert go over the steering wheel and throttle and develop my fingerprints. I suppose I'm in for it now."

Hal Anders, tall, sunburned, and ill at ease, came over to Mae Farr. "I'm sorry, Mae," he said simply.

She looked at him with troubled eyes.

"The D.A. has dismissed the case against me," Anders went on. "I don't know what that means."

"It means they're going to concentrate on me," she said.

"It was my gun they found there in the pipe," Anders said. "They thought Mason had planted it, but by checking up on the numbers, they found where the sale had been made directly to me, and they uncovered some other evidence. I don't know exactly what it is, but they've dropped the charge against me."

"That," she said, "is very nice. Congratulations. You seem to have saved yourself a disagreeable experience. Thanks to the advice of your very competent and very ethical family lawyer."

"Please, Mae, don't be like that."

She turned her face away from him.

Anders, conscious that the eyes of spectators were on him, knowing that reporters with high-speed lenses were surreptitiously clicking candid-camera shots, leaned forward until his lips were close to the ears of Mae Farr and Perry Mason. "Please don't, Mae," he said, "and listen, Mae. I did one thing for you. I did this on my own without *anyone's* advice. I managed to get in touch with Hazel Tooms this morning. She won't be here. She's on a plane to Mexico where a friend has a yacht. They're going to leave at once on a cruise for—and I quote—destination unknown."

Mae Farr's expression showed utter incredulity. "You did *that*?" she asked.

Mason's eyes hardened. They surveyed Anders with cold hostility. "I presume you realize," he said, "that I'll get the blame for that."

"No, you won't," Anders said quietly. "If it comes to a showdown, *I'll* take the blame."

Scanlon said, "I've already viewed the body of the deceased. The autopsy surgeon has pointed out the course of the bullet and the cause of death. It was a gunshot wound in the head. That much of the case is so clear that we don't have to waste the doctor's time in having him come down here."

He cleared his throat, glanced from Perry Mason to

Oscar Overmeyer, a deputy district attorney, and Carl Runcifer, who represented the district attorney's office. He said, "Proceedings are going to be short and informal. We're going to get at the facts. I don't want any delaying, technical objections from anyone to any of the testimony. I don't want any fancy legal arguments raised. If I think it will speed things along and help us get at the truth, I'll ask some of the questions myself. There isn't going to be any rambling cross-examination of witnesses just so the lawyers can make a showing of doing something; but if the attorneys for any of the interested parties want to ask questions purely for the purpose of clearing matters up, explaining or bringing out facts which the witnesses have neglected to state, I'm going to permit those questions."

Carl Runcifer started to make some objection to Scanlon's unorthodox procedures, but Overmeyer, who was familiar with Scanlon's temperament, pulled him back into his seat.

Judge Scanlon's clerk walked up to his informal podium and handed him a note. This gave Sidney Eversel time to march militantly over to Perry Mason. "I suppose," he said ominously, "you think you've been very, very clever."

"Now what?" Mason asked.

"I discovered the real object of your trip to my house early this morning," Eversel said. "I suppose you thought I'd keep my mouth shut and that you could blackmail me into doing almost anything you wanted in order to keep my connection with it a secret. For your information, I went at once to the police and notified the district attorney's office. I am advised that you were guilty of burglary in taking that negative. The only thing we lack is absolute proof. Produce that negative, Mr. Perry Mason, and you'll go to jail. *That* is where I stand." He turned on his heel and walked off.

Mason said to Mae Farr, "Well, you always claimed

that Anders was too conservative and wouldn't do anything without taking advice. He seems to have cut the apron strings with a very sharp pair of scissors. I'll leave you two for a few moments to fight it out."

He arose from his chair and walked back along the aisle of curious, staring spectators to engage in a whispered conference with Paul Drake and Della Street. "Called your office, Paul?"

"Yes, just a minute ago," Drake said. "I have a last-minute report, but it doesn't mean anything. I simply can't get anything on Hazel Tooms. She's apparently a playgirl who goes in for outdoor sports."

Mason said, "She told me all that herself. Where is she now, Paul?"

"She's under subpoena," Drake said, "and should be here. Good Lord, Perry, you haven't spirited her away, have you?"

Mason said, "No. Personally, I wish she were here."

"How are things looking?" Della asked in an anxious whisper.

Mason's eyes glinted with a frosty twinkle. "They look like hell, Della," he admitted. "Eversel got a burst of courage and went to the police, claimed the negative had been stolen, evidently told them all about taking the picture. That put Mae Farr right in the middle of a very hot spot. The police will now claim that she had a gun of her own, that she went back to the Yacht Club, took out Frank Marley's boat, overtook the *Penn*-went, killed Wentworth, returned to the Yacht Club, drove to the place where she'd seen Anders ditch the gun, and dropped the murder gun where it would be found as soon as the drainage waters evaporated."

"Isn't that going to make a strong case against her, Perry?" the detective asked.

"Very strong indeed," Mason said dryly. "I hadn't counted on Eversel overcoming his fear of publicity. Apparently, he's determined to get me. He reported the theft of the negative to the district attorney's office. Of course, the evidence about the taking of the picture gives them an entirely new slant on the case. They have left Anders out of it. They're concentrating on Mae Farr—and on me."

"Go to it, Chief," Della Street said. "Tear into them."

Mason grinned and said, "I don't know just how much tearing I can do. However, I have one ace up my sleeve. If I can play it at just the right time and in just the right manner, I can probably take the trick I want. If I can't, I'm hooked."

"What's the ace?" Drake asked.

"Just a hunch," Mason said. "I'm going to put a witness on the stand without knowing in advance what he's going to say. If he says the right thing, his very evident surprise will register with the J.P. Otherwise, it will look like a desperate attempt to drag a red herring across the trail."

Drake said, "Gosh, Perry, you did lay yourself wide open, going after that negative. Why the devil do you violate laws in order to get justice for your clients?"

Mason grinned and said, "I'll be damned if I know, Paul. I guess I'm just made that way. When I start unraveling a mystery, I can't seem to find a brake. Every time I put my foot down, it hits the throttle."

"I'll say it does," Drake agreed.

Della Street said calmly, "As a matter of fact, Chief, I was the one who took that negative out of the house. They can't get you for that."

Mason grinned and said, "You did it under my instructions, Della. You keep out of this."

"I will not," she retorted. "I'll take my share of the responsibility."

Emil Scanlon finished reading his note, whispered instructions to his secretary, and said, "Very well, we'll proceed with the preliminary hearing on the case of People against Mae Farr."

Oscar Overmeyer got to his feet. "May it please the Court," he said. "We understand your desire for an informal, expeditious hearing. However, within the last few hours, I may say within the last few minutes, the district attorney's office has come into possession of evidence which materially changes the entire complexion of the case.

"We are now prepared to show by witnesses that the murder did not take place as was originally supposed. In fact, we might refer to it as the case of the postponed murder. What Harold Anders really believed to have been a shot and what Mae Farr said she believed was a shot was in reality not a shot, but the explosion of a flash bulb.

"We understand, of course, that the Justice wishes to move this hearing along as fast as possible. For that reason, we call our first witness, Sidney Eversel, and call the Justice's attention to the fact that the testimony of this witness will be so pertinent, in fact I may say so spectacular, as to cause a complete change in our order of calling other witnesses."

Scanlon frowned a moment in thought, glanced surreptitiously at Perry Mason, saw no evidence of an objection, and said, "Very well, for the purpose of getting to the bottom of this case in the shortest possible time, I'll let you call Sidney Eversel."

Sidney Eversel marched forward and was sworn.

"Do you," Scanlon asked, "know anything about this murder?"

"I know this much about it," Eversel said. "I know when it was *not* committed."

"Exactly what do you know?" the Justice asked.

Sidney Eversel said, "I'm going to make a clean breast of things. I have long been in love with Juanita Wentworth. I met her and fell in love with her while she was still married to Penn Wentworth, while she was living with him as his wife. The intensity of my emotion made me indiscreet."

Eversel paused and swallowed. Evidently he had memorized this much of his testimony but found the recital of it more difficult than he had anticipated. After a moment, he went on, "Wentworth was diabolically clever. He found out all about our affair. I believe he was insanely jealous of me. He wanted Juanita—Mrs. Wentworth—to return to him. She had left him shortly after meeting me. He threatened that unless she did return, he would sue me for alienation of affections. He refused to give her a divorce. His entire actions were those of a man who is utterly selfish and acting without consideration."

"Never mind that," Scanlon interrupted. "Just what do you know?"

Eversel said, "I rankled at the injustice of it because I knew that Wentworth was entertaining numerous women aboard his yacht. I determined to get evidence which would put Wentworth on the defensive—in a position where he would be forced to listen to reason and give his wife a divorce without dragging my name into it."

"What did you do?" Scanlon asked.

"On the night of the twelfth," Eversel said, "I lay in wait at the Yacht Club watching his boat. I knew that Miss Farr had been a frequent visitor aboard that yacht. The night was hot and stuffy. Wentworth had the skylight in his cabin open. I crept closer and closer to the yacht, listening. When I thought the time was ripe, I boarded the yacht and looked down through the skylight. I saw Wentworth in a very compromising position. His face was away from the camera. I put my finger on the shutter release and called his name softly. He didn't hear me the first time. I called a second time, and he looked up in alarm. At that moment, I pressed the trigger and a flash bulb, synchronized with the shutter of the camera, exploded, giving me a sharp, clear picture."

"What did you do?"

Carl Runcifer whispered to Oscar Overmeyer, "This is the most incredible substitute for a legal proceeding imaginable. Are you going to let Scanlon get by with this type of hearing? Aren't you going to object to his examining the witnesses?"

"Won't do a bit of good," Overmeyer whispered back. "This is the way Emil Scanlon always runs his show; and surprisingly enough, it always comes out okay."

"I turned and ran from the yacht," Eversel continued. "I drove home and developed the picture. It was a perfect negative. I could hardly wait. I knew that Mrs. Wentworth was in San Diego. I jumped in my plane and flew to San Diego, explained the circumstances to her, and brought her back with me. By the time we returned, the negative was dry. I put it in the enlarging camera and made a print. Naturally I felt very jubilant. Then I flew Mrs. Wentworth back to San Diego.

"Subsequently, that negative was stolen from my house. At the time of its disappearance, Perry Mason, the attorney representing Miss Farr, was prowling around the grounds. I demand that that negative be produced. When it is produced, I intend to prosecute him for burglary."

Emil Scanlon pursed his lips thoughtfully and assiduously avoided glancing at Perry Mason. "Well," he said after a moment, "if anything like that happened, it's something that's entirely apart from this case. As I see it, your testimony may show that the murder wasn't committed at the time we had supposed. That's all that relates to the present investigation."

Oscar Overmeyer said, "May I ask a question if the Justice please?"

"Yes."

"When you were flying to San Diego the first time,"

Overmeyer asked, "did you take a direct course a part of the way over the water?"

"Yes," Eversel answered. "My plane is an amphibian. The night was calm. The rainstorm hadn't begun then, and the safety factor in night flying induced me to keep over the ocean."

"While you were near the outer entrance of the harbor, did you notice by any chance a yacht?"

"I did."

"What yacht was it?"

"It was the express cruiser *Atina* belonging to Frank Marley."

"And who is Frank Marley?"

"A partner of Wentworth's."

"You know him?"

"I know of him, and I know him personally. I am quite familiar with his boat."

"You were flying low?"

"Yes."

"What did you do, if anything?"

"I circled the cruiser several times, thinking that it was rather significant that it was heading out to sea."

"Did you have any means of illumination by which you could . . ."

"Yes, I have a pair of searchlights in the wings. I turned them on the cruiser."

"What did you see?"

"I identified the *Atina* absolutely. I saw that someone was at the wheel. I could see that someone was a woman, and that she was wearing clothes of the identical color that had been worn by Mae Farr when she went aboard the Pennwent earlier in the evening."

Overmeyer bowed and smiled. "If the Justice please," he said, "that is all."

Mason raised his eyebrows at the J.P., and Emil Scanlon nodded.

"Did you fly over any other yachts while you were en route to San Diego?" Mason asked casually.

Overmeyer said, "If the Justice please, that has nothing to do with this case. It is an attempt to confuse the issues and—"

"I would have asked the question myself if Mr. Mason hadn't," the J.P. interrupted. "I said I didn't want any purely technical objections. Let's hear the answer to that question."

Eversel squirmed uneasily in the witness chair. He glanced appealingly at Overmeyer, then averted his eyes.

"Answer the question," Emil Scanlon said, his voice taking on the edge of authority, like a ballplayer telling the umpire that he missed the last call.

"Well," Eversel said, "naturally in taking a course for San Diego, I was flying on just about the course a ship would have taken in going to Ensenada."

"Never mind the explanations," Scanlon said. "You can make those later. The question was whether you flew over any other yachts."

"Yes, I did."

"Did you," Scanlon asked, "recognize any of those yachts?"

"I recognized one of them."

"Was it the *Pennwent?*" Scanlon asked sternly.

Eversel kept his eyes straight ahead. "Yes, it was," he said in a strained voice.

"And did you circle over her?"

"Just once."

"What did you see?"

"I saw her plugging along with the skylight in the cabin open."

"Was there anyone at the wheel?" Scanlon asked.

"I don't think this witness could see that distinctly," Overmeyer objected. "It's asking rather much . . ."

"No, it isn't," Scanlon said. "A witness who could look

at one yacht and testify to the color of the clothes worn by the person at the wheel could certainly see if anyone was at the steering wheel of another yacht. Answer that question, Mr. Eversel."

Eversel said, "No one was at the wheel."

"You only circled the yacht once?"

"Yes."

"Are you certain no one was at the wheel?"

"Yes."

"Where was the yacht then?"

"About a mile off shore and about ten miles below the breakwater."

"And how far from Frank Marley's boat?" Mason asked.

"About three miles, I should judge."

Mason said, in a very conversational tone of voice, "You knew that Wentworth had a violent temper, didn't you, Mr. Eversel?"

"I did."

"And you knew that if he caught you aboard the *Pennwent,* he might resort to violence?"

"Yes."

"You knew he was a powerful man?"

"Yes."

"I suppose," Mason said, "that's why you went armed."

"Well, I carried a weapon. I didn't propose——" The witness suddenly broke off as the full significance of Mason's question dawned upon him.

"And saw no reason for removing that weapon before you stepped into your airplane?"

"To tell you the truth, I forgot all about it."

"So that at the time you were circling over Wentworth's yacht, you were armed. Is that right?"

"I don't like the way you put that question."

"Never mind whether you like it or not," Scanlon said. "Answer it."

"Yes, I was," Eversel snapped.

"What kind of a revolver?"

"A thirty-eight—a Colt."

Mason smiled affably. "That," he said, "is all."

Scanlon frowned. "I am not certain that I care to have the examination concluded at just this point," he said. "Well, perhaps we'll let the matter rest temporarily. You'll remain in attendance, Mr. Eversel."

"Just one more question," Mason asked. "You stated that you made an enlargement of that negative, Mr. Eversel?"

"I did."

"Where is it?"

"I gave it to the deputy district attorney."

"Mr. Overmeyer?"

"No, Mr. Runcifer."

Mason smiled. "Would you mind producing that print, Mr. Runcifer?"

Runcifer said, "I certainly would. That's a part of the confidential files of the district attorney's office. I object to any such a demand. If you want that photograph in evidence, produce it yourself, and when you do so, account for the fact that you have that negative in your possession."

Emil Scanlon, in a voice that was suavely courteous, said, "If there are no more questions of Mr. Eversel, he will be excused. But remain in attendance."

Eversel left the witness stand.

Runcifer exchanged a triumphant glance with his associate.

"And now," Overmeyer said, "we will call Hazel Tooms as our next witness."

"Thank you very much," Scanlon said, "but the Justice has his own ideas about who should be the next witness. Mr. Runcifer, will you please come forward and be sworn?"

"Me?" Runcifer exclaimed. "I most strenuously object on the ground—"

Scanlon nodded affably and cut Runcifer in midsentence. ". . . Just step right up to the witness stand, Mr. Runcifer."

Oscar Overmeyer said in a loud half-whisper: "You'd better go if you don't want a contempt citation. This guy means business."

Runcifer moved slowly forward, held up his hand, and was sworn.

Emil Scanlon said, "Do you have in your possession a photograph which purports to be a print of the flashlight photograph taken by the witness who last testified?"

"Your Honor, I object to that," Oscar Overmeyer said. "That is a part of the—"

"I don't want any objections," Scanlon said. "I want that photograph if you have it."

There was a moment of tense, dramatic silence. Then Runcifer said, "Very much against my wishes and over my protests, I produce the photograph the Justice of the Peace has requested." Runcifer could not keep a condescending tone out of his voice when he said "justice of the peace."

He opened his briefcase and took out an enlargement on glossy paper which he handed to the Justice. At the same time he favored Perry Mason with a glance of savage hostility.

"While we're about it," Scanlon said casually, "you seem to have a lot of other photographs there. What are they, pictures showing the interior of the *Pennwent?*"

"Yes."

"Let's have them," Scanlon said.

Runcifer took out a series of pictures, explaining that they showed the posture of the body when it was discovered, the interior of the cabin when the yacht had been brought in, the exterior of the yacht, the yacht in its berth at the Yacht Club, and an airplane view of the club showing the floats to which boats were moored. Scanlon marked them all in numerical order

177

and announced them as exhibits. "That's all, Mr. Runcifer," he said. "Thank you."

Runcifer stalked stiffly back to his seat.

"Well," Scanlon said, "let's hear from Hazel Tooms. Will you come forward and be sworn, please?"

There was a craning of necks, but no rustle of motion usual when a witness moves toward the witness box.

Scanlon frowned and said, "Wasn't she under subpoena?"

Runcifer said acidly, "She was under subpoena. She stated that at least one attempt had been made to get her to leave the country. When she was subpoenaed, we believe she was about to put herself beyond the jurisdiction of the court."

"I'm not concerned with that," Emil Scanlon said. "We're holding only one postmortem, and that's on the death of Wentworth and the probable involvement of the accused, Mae Farr. The question is, where is this witness now?"

"I don't know," Runcifer said.

Scanlon's eyes turned to Perry Mason and became suddenly stern. "Mr. Mason," he said, "I think I'll now ask you to take the stand."

Mason obediently took the witness stand, realizing that any protest would be quickly overruled.

"Do you know this witness, Hazel Tooms?" Emil Scanlon asked.

"I do."

"Did you talk with her about the case?"

"I did."

"Do you know where she is now?"

"I do not."

"Do you know how she happened to leave?"

"Not of my own knowledge, no."

"Were you directly or indirectly responsible for her departure?"

"No."

"That's all," the Justice said.

Runcifer said eagerly, "I'd like to ask this witness one or two questions."

Scanlon hesitated a moment, then said, "I didn't give him an opportunity to ask you any questions."

"This is different," Runcifer said.

"I'll hear the question and see if I permit it," Scanlon said.

"When you talked with Miss Tooms, wasn't the subject discussed that she might leave the country for a financial consideration, and didn't you discuss with her the amount of money necessary?"

"You might put it that way," Mason said calmly. "She made the proposition. I turned it down."

"Oh," Runcifer said, his voice filled with sarcasm. "You went to her apartment. She told you that she had testimony which would be very damaging to your client, and offered to leave the country, and you were too ethical to even entertain such a proposition. Is that the idea you wish to convey?"

Scanlon said, "You don't have to answer that question, Mr. Mason. Now then, Mr. Runcifer, we're not going to have any more such bursts of sarcasm from Counsel. We're here to try and find out whether there's enough evidence to hold this accused for trial in Superior Court for the murder of Penn Wentworth. That's all. You can air your grievances some other place than in my courtroom."

Mason said, "Begging Your Honor's pardon, I'd like to answer the question."

"Go ahead," the Justice said.

Mason crossed his long legs in front of him, smiled down at Runcifer, and said, "Your question assumes an erroneous fact, Mr. Runcifer. The testimony which Hazel Tooms was to have given, in place of being detrimental to my client, was really most advantageous. I regret that she isn't here."

"All right," Runcifer said triumphantly. "Since you've opened the door as to the nature of her testimony, I'll ask you this question. I assume the Justice will admit it. He's let in everything else. Isn't it a fact that she said she had gone to the Yacht Club to call on Wentworth, that Wentworth had advised her he was going to Ensenada that night and asked her to go along, that she went back to get some groceries and some clothes, and when she returned, the yacht was gone, that she waited for some time, and while she was waiting, she saw Frank Marley's boat come in to its landing, that she watched to see who had been piloting that boat, and that the only person who left it was Mae Farr, your client."

"That," Mason said calmly, "is substantially what she said."

"And you consider that that is to the advantage of your client?" Runcifer asked.

Mason nodded gravely. "I do."

There was a moment's astonished silence, followed by a whispered conference on the part of the deputy district attorneys.

Scanlon said, "I guess that's all, Mr. Mason. I think that's all the examination I'll permit anyway. You may leave the stand."

Mason returned to his chair.

Runcifer got to his feet and said, almost pleadingly, "Won't the Justice permit me to ask Mr. Mason one more question?"

"I don't think so," Scanlon said. "You seem to have covered the situation pretty well. What was the question you wanted to ask?"

"I wanted to ask Mr. Mason just how he could possibly claim that that testimony was of any advantage to his client."

Scanlon shook his head. "That would mean just a lot of argument," he said.

Mason, from his chair, said, "I think perhaps if Your

Honor permitted that question and I answered it, it might clear up a lot of misunderstandings right now."

"Go ahead and answer it," Scanlon said. "To be perfectly frank, I'm interested in the answer although I consider the question somewhat improper and an attempt to take advantage of a witness who apparently has been very fair and frank. Go ahead and answer it, Mr. Mason."

Mason walked up to Scanlon's bench where the photographs were spread out and said, "In answering that question, it's going to be necessary to correlate certain facts at some length."

"Go ahead and correlate them," Scanlon invited "That's what we're here for. Just make it terse and logical and keep within the facts, and we'll listen. We don't want to hear any impassioned argument."

"I'm not going to make any," Mason said with a smile.

"Go ahead," Scanlon invited, "and answer the question."

Mason said, "I think the tag which was given to this case by learned counsel for the prosecution is perhaps the best description of the case. Your Honor will remember that he referred to it as 'The Case of the Postponed Murder.'

"Quite obviously, Penn Wentworth was shot from a distance. There are no powder marks on his clothing or on his body. He was evidently shot from above, as Your Honor knows from talking to the autopsy surgeon. It is quite natural to suppose that he was shot through the skylight of his yacht by someone who was well above him, a distance, let us say, that was not less than six or eight feet and which stretches indefinitely into space as far as anyone could have accurately aimed a gun and fired a bullet. For instance, I believe that Mr. Eversel is an expert revolver shot and has acquired some reputation as an authority on firearms. I believe that's correct, Mr. Eversel?"

Eversel hesitated and nodded curtly.

"Your Honor, if we're still taking testimony, I suggest that witness Eversel be asked to return to the witness box," Runcifer exploded.

"You let me worry about that, won't you?" Scanlon said evenly.

Mason continued: "And you would back the statement I have just made from your knowledge of the case and your experience with firearms?"

Eversel made no move to answer. Mason went on affably, "Well, it's of no moment. I merely mentioned it so that we can keep in mind the position of the person who fired the shot and the position of the man who was the target.

"Now let's examine the possibilities. Let's first consider Anders. He could hardly have committed the murder. The evidence shows that Wentworth's yacht was only a couple of miles ahead of Marley's cruiser when Eversel saw them. Wentworth had much the slower boat. However, making all due allowances for speed, it would seem quite apparent that Wentworth must have pulled out with his yacht very shortly after Mae Farr and Anders drove away, perhaps within half an hour. Anders says that he threw his gun away. Mae Farr also testifies to that. The evidence shows that the murder gun was found. It certainly wasn't the gun Anders had or was carrying. Moreover, Anders went to the city and almost immediately started for North Mesa, and I understand that the police have been able to trace his movements so that they are convinced he didn't return to the Yacht Club after his conversation with me.

"Miss Farr and I drove to the Yacht Club. We found the *Pennwent* gone. We returned and Miss Farr stayed with me until after I had passed the place where Anders threw the gun. She then doubled back and took Marley's cruiser."

"You're admitting that?" Runcifer asked incredulously.

"Of course I'm admitting it," Mason said. "Now let's look at it from her viewpoint. Suppose she had gone out and overtaken Wentworth's yacht, as could well have happened. She couldn't have put the *Atina* alongside the *Pennwent* without Wentworth's knowing it was there. It's a physical impossibility to do that without bumping or jarring. Moreover, she couldn't have kept her boat at cruising speed, laid her alongside the *Pennwent*, left the wheel, and made fast to Wentworth's yacht without help. She would have required either that Wentworth slow down or that someone help her, or both.

"However, suppose that Wentworth did slow down, suppose that Mae Farr boarded the *Pennwent*. Wentworth would have had to help her. They could have gone down to the cabin together. Wentworth had an automatic pilot on his yacht. There was no necessity for him to be at the wheel. But there is no likely combination of circumstances by which he could have been in the cabin and Miss Farr could have stood on the deck and shot him through the open skylight.

"Let's take the case of Eversel. He is an aviator. He flew low over the yacht. He was armed. He's an expert shot. But before I go into that, I want to call your attention to a significant item in these photographs. Notice the photograph which was taken by Eversel. I want to call Your Honor's attention to this little shelf. You will notice a circular object in a case with a cylindrical object near it."

Runcifer got to his feet and walked quickly to the Justice's bench to examine what Mason was pointing out. "That," Runcifer said, "is a rare coin. Wentworth was a prominent collector of rare coins."

"Quite possibly," Mason said. "And with a magnifying glass you can notice certain distinctive marks on this coin. There are two parallel lines with interlacing, diagonal lines in between them."

The Justice studied it through the magnifying glass. "Just how is that significant, Mr. Mason?" he asked.

"One moment, Your Honor," Mason said. "Examine this picture of the cabin taken through the skylight by the police after the *Pennwent* was returned. There is the same shelf. But the objects are missing."

Scanlon nodded.

"Now then," Mason said, "we are confronted with this situation. Whatever those objects were, they were on the *Pennwent* when Eversel took that flashlight photograph. As soon as that photograph was taken, Eversel left the yacht. Wentworth ran back to the after cabin. Miss Farr ran out on deck and joined Anders. The two of them left the yacht together. There's no evidence showing that Eversel, Anders, or Mae Farr ever returned to that yacht.

"But here are two objects clearly shown in one photograph and clearly absent from a subsequent photograph. Why? Where did they go? Who took them?"

Scanlon said, "You have some theory about that, Mr. Mason?"

"I have," Mason said. "I'd like to call one witness."

"Well, I don't know that the State has rested," Overmeyer said hesitantly in hopeless confusion.

"Oh, what does that matter when we're trying to clear up this case?" Scanlon said. "Go ahead, Mason. Call whoever you want to."

"Mr. Robert Grastin," Mason announced.

A tall skinny man with sunken eyes, thin lips, and high cheekbones came forward. He was in his early fifties, a man with long arms and legs, quiet and unhurried in his manner. He said, "I hate to disappoint people, but I don't know one single thing about this case. I don't know any of the parties."

Mason said, "That's quite all right. Just take the stand, and we'll see what you know, Mr. Grastin."

Grastin slipped into the witness chair.

Mason said, "I believe the subpoena that was served on you called for you to bring certain records with you."

"Yes."

"Now just so the Justice can get the picture," Mason said, "kindly explain to him who you are and what your occupation is."

Grastin said, "I am the secretary and treasurer of the Interurban Amateur Athletic League. That is an association of amateur athletes sponsored by an interurban busline for the purpose of promoting civic relations and—"

"And traffic?" Mason interrupted with a smile.

"And traffic," Grastin admitted. "The theory being that interurban matches are arranged at places which are most advantageously reached by the interurban service. Prizes are awarded. Competition is encouraged, and the line receives a certain amount of advertising."

"Now then, on the twelfth," Mason said, "you sponsored certain athletic activities?"

"Yes, sir. On the twelfth, the open tennis tournament reached the stage of finals."

"And on that day," Mason asked, "do your records show who won second place in the women's division?"

"*Second* place?" Grastin asked.

Mason nodded.

"Just a moment," Grastin said, and took from his pocket a leather-backed notebook filled with typewritten sheets of paper. He ran down the page to which he had opened the book, and said, "Our records show that second place was won by Miss Hazel Tooms who resides in the Balkan Apartments."

"Exactly," Mason said. "Now, I am interested in going back over the records of other athletic activities. Do you have an alphabetical index showing the names of winners?"

"We do."

"That is with you?"

"It's in my briefcase."

"Get it, please."

Grastin walked to his seat in the front of the room, picked up a briefcase, returned with it to the witness stand, and took out a large looseleaf notebook.

"Look under the name of Tooms," Mason said, "and see what else you find."

Grastin ran through the pages. Suddenly he said, "Wait a minute. I remember that name now. She's won quite a few championships; she's quite an all-round athlete."

"All right," Mason said. "Just look through your records. Now, what do you find in connection with swimming?"

"In each of the past two years," Grastin said, "she has won the women's long-distance swimming championship. Last year, she also won the four-hundred-meter free-style swimming event for women. In—"

"I think that's enough," Mason said. "It's enough to prove my point in any event. Now, I'm going to show you this photograph, Mr. Grastin, and call your attention to a coinlike object contained in a case and shown on this shelf." Mason handed him the photograph and pointed. "Please look at it with this magnifying glass. Can you tell what it is?"

Grastin held the magnifying glass in position, then said slowly, "Why, yes. That's the medal we had struck off for second place in the women's tennis tournament. That series of lines across it represents a tennis net."

Mason smiled affably at Justice of the Peace Scanlon and said, "I think, Your Honor, by the time the district attorney's office puts two and two together, it will have an answer to its question of who killed Penn Wentworth; and it wasn't Mae Farr."

13

MASON, Della Street, Mae Farr, and Paul Drake sat in Mason's office. Mae Farr seemed dazed at the swift turn of events. "I don't see how you figured it out," she said. "I thought I was up against a certain conviction."

Mason said, "It was mighty thin ice. Almost as soon as I talked with Hazel Tooms, I sensed she was altogether too eager to get out of the country. My first reaction was that her eagerness was due to the fact that her apartment had been bugged and the police were trying to trap me. When she saw I wasn't walking into the trap, she tried too hard to get me in.

"Later events caused me to change that opinion. If, then, her anxiety to escape hadn't been a scheme to trap me, what *was* the cause? That opened up an interesting field of speculation. I knew that she was an all-round athlete. I could tell by looking at her, and she had told me of winning second place in that tennis tournament. I also sensed that she had really cared a great deal for Penn Wentworth, and I believe, though I can't prove it, that theirs was more than a platonic friendship.

"It was quite obvious to me that Wentworth either must have been shot from an airplane or by someone who had been aboard the *Pennwent* with him and had been able to swim ashore after the shooting.

"I knew that Marley's alibi wasn't cast-iron, but he didn't impress me as being a man who could have swum ashore, landed virtually naked, and made his way back to the hospital without showing some evidence of his experience. Mrs. Wentworth might have done it, but it was quite evident that she was in San Diego. Unless Eversel had shot Wentworth from the airplane, I couldn't connect him with it. You were out in Marley's boat. You brought it back. For the reasons I mentioned, I didn't think you could have done the actual killing.

"As soon as I realized that what you had taken for the flash of a pistol was probably the release of a flashlight bulb, I knew that the murder had been postponed from that moment until a later one.

"Once I had that theory, it was easy to reconstruct what must have happened. Hazel Tooms won the second-place medal in the tennis finals. She went down to Wentworth's yacht to be congratulated. Knowing what we do of Wentworth, we can be sure that his idea of congratulations would require the use of lipstick by Hazel Tooms after those congratulations were received. When she had repaired the damage, she put the medal and the lipstick on the shelf in the cabin.

"Wentworth then told her of his plan to sail to Ensenada that night and asked her if she'd like to go with him. She was delighted but pointed out that she'd have to get some clothes and that they needed some provisions. So she left the *Pennwent*, drove home to pack, and on the way back stopped to pick up the provisions.

"During the time she was gone, you, Mae, boarded the *Pennwent* and had your struggle with Wentworth. Eversel boarded the boat and took the photograph of Wentworth in a compromising position, then left. Anders boarded the boat to rescue you. Then you two left.

"Some time after that, probably not long after, Hazel Tooms returned with the provisions, boarded the *Pennwent*, and she and Wentworth set sail for Ensenada.

"Wentworth was undoubtedly angry and upset. He knew he had been photographed. He reacted instinctively by doubling up and covering his face. He could guess that that photograph might make it very much more difficult for him to arrange a divorce on reasonable terms when he met his wife the next morning. He probably told Hazel Tooms all about it.

"Whether or not Wentworth had promised to marry Hazel if and when he got his freedom, I think Hazel assumed that was his intention and he made it plain that was a ridiculous assumption. For whatever reason, she was filled with murderous rage. He was probably sitting there laughing at her when she pulled the gun and shot him.

"She thought she'd killed him outright. The impact of the bullet must have knocked him out before he came to and wandered around. And she had to get off the boat. I believe she carried one of those canvas bags people take aboard instead of suitcases—just as I believe she always carried a gun in case one of the yachtsmen she picked up got too rough. I think she took off her clothes, stuffed them in the bag along with the swimming medal, the lipstick, and the gun, set the automatic pilot on the course for Ensenada if that hadn't already been done, dove overboard with the bag, and swam ashore.

"At first, I couldn't understand why she would have taken along the murder weapon instead of dumping it overboard. Then I put myself in her place and realized what she was up against. She'd arrive on shore naked at some strange place. She'd have to put on her wet clothes and find some motorist who would pick her up as a hitchhiker and take her to within walking distance of the Yacht Club where she had left her car. As a matter of protection, she decided to keep her revolver with her.

"She got back to the Yacht Club in time to see Mae Farr coming in aboard the *Atina*. Then she went home. The next morning, in the news coverage of the murder, she learned where Anders had thrown his gun. She drove down and 'planted' the murder weapon. Sometime that morning she also told Frank Marley about seeing Mae Farr bringing in the *Atina*."

"That's quite a reconstruction, Perry," Paul Drake said, "but I still don't see how you can figure that a normal, well-balanced, athletic girl like Hazel Tooms would commit murder."

"She might have fooled me if it hadn't been for one thing, Paul."

"What's that?"

"No matter what other facts we may get by surmise, one fact stands out as absolutely true. The person who killed Wentworth took the murder weapon down to the place where Anders had thrown his gun and planted it in hopes that it would clinch the case against Anders. In other words, the murderer was quite willing to send Anders up for a life sentence or a death penalty for a crime he hadn't committed. That showed that the person who had done the killing knew that there was some possibility a subsequent investigation might be made, that that person might be suspected, and strove to forestall both the investigation and the suspicion by deliberately trying to build up an iron-clad case against Anders."

"That," Drake said, "is right."

"What'll they do with her?" Mae Farr asked.

Mason said, "Well, that depends. First, they'll have to catch her, which I don't think will be easy. Then, they'll have to convict her, and that's going to be quite a job. That photograph Eversel took will come pretty close to getting her an acquittal if she testifies that Wentworth made the same sort of attack on her that he made on you."

"Planting that gun will look like the devil as far as her case is concerned," Drake said.

Mason grinned and said, "In one way, yes, but—oh come on, Paul, you can't convict a woman with a figure like hers of anything worse than manslaughter."

"How about Eversel?" Drake asked.

"He shook hands and made up," Mason said. "He was

so darned afraid I was going to accuse him of the murder and make it stick that the real solution came as a a great relief to him. He'd been scared stiff. Moreover, when he realized that because of my activities, an innocent woman had been liberated, he began to think I wasn't such a bad egg after all. In fact, Della, he's invited us down for dinner next week."

"Are we going?" she asked.

"Why not?" Mason asked. "In the meantime, let's climb in the car and go places."

"Where?" she asked.

"Oh, take a trip," Mason said. "Why not drive up toward North Mesa and look that country over?"

"Would you risk it?" Mae Farr asked.

"Risk what?"

"You'll probably come to blows with Hal's family lawyer."

"Fiddlesticks," Mason said. "I have no feelings like that. Actually the man was right."

"Well," she said, "I'm going that way myself this afternoon."

"You *are*?" Della asked in surprise.

She nodded.

Mason said, "Well, well, well! How did that happen?"

She flushed and said spiritedly, "It's a woman's prerogative to change her mind, isn't it? Maybe I've changed mine about Hal."

Mason said, "He does seem to have developed a lot of independence lately."

Mae Farr laughed nervously. "Yes. He's picked up quite a few ideas of his own. I think this murder case may have been a good thing—for him. I wish you would come and have dinner with us tomorrow night, Mr. Mason. It's going to be a special occasion."

Mason looked at Mae Farr with a twinkle in his eyes. "A sort of celebration?" he asked.

She nodded. "I'm going to tell Hal I'll marry him."

191

"Good girl!" Mason said, then he turned to Della Street. "How about it, Della?"

"Leaving it up to me, Chief?"

He nodded.

"Let's go to North Mesa," she said, "if you *really* want us, Miss Farr."

"Oh, but I really do," Mae Farr said eagerly.

Paul Drake got to his feet, fed a stick of gum into his mouth, and said, "Well, nice to have known you."

"Aren't you coming, too, Mr. Drake?" Mae Farr asked.

"Not me," Drake said. "When wedding bells ring the enthusiasm is apt to be contagious. What would a detective do with a wife?"

"Wrong again," Mason said cheerfully. "What would a wife do with a detective?"

Drake paused in the outer doorway for a parting shot. "Particularly a detective who works for a lawyer who keeps him up all night, running around committing felonies," he said, and punctuated his remark by banging the door shut behind him.